Praise for
In the Shadow of Green Bamboos

"Few writers have the graceful and poetic sensitivity to ponder the past and allow it to bubble to the surface with the serendipity that C. L. Hoang continues to gift us in his writings. His life experiences, of being born in Vietnam and witnessing the war there, then moving to the United States to live, enable him to reflect the impact of time, cultures, and memories in this striking collection of stories, *In the Shadow of Green Bamboos*. Revolving around the family and the bonding that grows out of dark times into moments of light, these stories journey back and forth between war-torn Vietnam and the U.S., and between the now and the then—a veritable Pandora's Box of gems that invite introspection and healing."

> —Grady Harp, MD, author of *War Songs: Metaphors in Clay and Poetry from the Vietnam Experience*, Amazon Hall-of-Fame reviewer, Goodreads Top-50 reviewer

"C. L. Hoang is a superb storyteller who weaves deeply emotional tales enhanced by rich memories of his childhood in Vietnam. He has a gift for describing a setting in such a way that one can almost taste the mung bean cookies, breathe the heavy, damp air of the monsoon season, or feel the vibration through the ground of bomb chains striking near Saigon. Yet the families and villages strive to carry on, with themes of love and family underpinning each story in this memorable collection, *In the Shadow of Green Bamboos*. For one who grew up in America during the 1960's, these stories, set in both Vietnam and the U.S., resonated powerfully. Be sure to have plenty of tissues on hand."

—Lynne M. Spreen, award-winning author of *Dakota Blues*

"C. L. Hoang sensitively traces the effects of the Vietnam War on a handful of characters—former soldiers, refugees, and their children. Each story is a complete and haunting tale of loss, grief, and resilience, but some of the stories also pick up characters from his published novel *Once upon a Mulberry Field*, giving us a glimpse into their future. His understanding of the inner lives of children is particularly keen."

—Margaret Diehl, author of *The Boy on the Green Bicycle*

In the Shadow of Green Bamboos

Stories

C. L. HOANG

Willow Stream Publishing
San Diego

In the Shadow of Green Bamboos
by C. L. Hoang

Published in the United States by Willow Stream Publishing
willowstreampublishing@gmail.com

ISBN (Paperback): 978-0-9899756-2-9

Library of Congress Control Number: 2020909987

Cover Design and Interior Layout: Nick Zelinger

First Edition

Printed in the United States of America

By C. L. Hoàng

Fiction

In the Shadow of Green Bamboos

Once upon a Mulberry Field

Nonfiction

Rain Falling on Tamarind Trees

In the Shadow
of Green Bamboos

People are trapped in history and history is trapped in them.
—James Baldwin

For the dead and the living, we must bear witness.
—Elie Wiesel

Contents

My village lies by a green bamboo hedge
Tucked in a bend of the Tô-Lịch River
With trees of fruit growing on the two banks
And schools of fish splashing in the water

—Vietnamese folk lullaby

Preface

Back when I was writing *Once upon a Mulberry Field*, my novel about the Việt-Nam War, I was confronted with the difficult task of choosing which material to include in the book. There was so much about the war that had been left untold due to the controversial and political nature of the subject, which made any attempt to bridge the gap a challenging endeavor. Even at nearly four hundred pages, my book barely scratches the surface of my own memory of those turbulent times. It was an impossible task to select among events that I had direct knowledge of as a child growing up in Việt-Nam and countless others that I heard or read about secondhand in later years. Those accounts of devastation and survival, part of the oral history of the times, were so compelling they burrowed deep into the nooks and crannies of my young mind. There, they have remained, tucked away, dormant at times but never forgotten.

In 2016, after a forty-year absence, I went back to Việt-Nam to visit for the first time. Upon returning to the U.S., my head still buzzing with vivid memories of the ancestral homeland, I set out to recapture the journey in a travelogue titled *Rain Falling on Tamarind Trees*. But as I was grinding away at the new project, I felt the old stories tugging hard at me again, in particular the ones that had been left out of *Mulberry Field*. Fueled by the once-familiar sights and sounds rediscovered during the trip, they had now re-emerged in burnished detail to occupy my thoughts and would not let go. More urgently than ever before, these long-buried stories were clamoring for an outlet—a voice. No longer would they be swept under the rug of time. Hence my decision, then and there, to make them the central theme of my next writing project after the travelogue.

In the meantime, perhaps not surprisingly, I had begun to feel twinges of nostalgia for the characters in *Mulberry Field*. After all, having worked with them for hours every day during the six-year gestation of the book, I had come to view them as more than friends. Together, we had shared momentous events in their lives as well as their fears and hopes, loves, and losses. I had been privy to their innermost thoughts and feelings and had felt great empathy for them, as I would for members of my own family. And so, occasionally, I found myself wandering back among the pages of *Mulberry Field* for a sentimental visit with my old friends. It also happened that I was hearing from readers who had missed the characters, much as I had, and that sparked an idea in my head. What if I were to bring back the characters in *Mulberry Field*, accompanied by new ones, and let them tell the stories that I had in store for my next book?

The idea started brewing in the back of my mind. It became even more pressing after *Rain Falling on Tamarind Trees* was published. Without preconceived notions or much forethought, I began to nibble at the new project and experiment with it. It took trial and error, using various approaches, before I could settle on a sensible way to go about it. And after numerous starts and stops, further hampered by a series of distractions that sent me off on diverging paths, the new book, at long last, is seeing the light of day.

This time, however, you will not witness the characters facing imminent danger or death day in and day out, alongside each other. For better or worse, the war has ended, at least on the battlefield. They have returned to their "regular" lives, trying to pick up where they had left off and move on as best they can. It is from this personal perspective that they will each share their struggle—a silent and lonely one, though no less harrowing or inspiring—to cope with the war's aftermath and the burden of the past. I discovered in the process of writing that these unique tales of resilience and courage lend themselves more naturally to the short-story format. This is because they stand alone as snapshots in the life of an individual, rather than being part of a larger story that covers multiple characters over a period of time, as is often the case in a novel.

The result is this collection of six stories, each of them a fictionalized amalgamation of real-life anecdotes, personal memories, and childhood dreams and reminiscence. Despite sharing the common backdrop of war, these stories mostly focus on revealing the blessings of love and hope in the course of every-day life. In addition, three of the six involve some familiar characters from *Once upon a Mulberry Field* to form, one might say, a mini-sequel to it. But readers who have not read the novel need not be concerned, as the stories are self-contained, and all the characters' backgrounds fully defined.

One of my favorite quotes from contemporary fiction is uttered by the narrator in Kristin Hannah's *The Nightingale*: "If I have learned anything in this long life of mine, it is this: in love we find out who we want to be; in war we find out who we are."

On that note, I invite you to come along, and let's see if together we can't find out who the true persons are behind the characters in this book. I hope you will enjoy the discovery.

C. L. Hoàng

In a Land Called Honah-Lee

The day began to fade, lifting away some of the oppressive heat and mugginess of a July afternoon in the capital city. The throngs of daytime visitors had thinned out, with only a few stragglers left behind dragging themselves through the deepening twilight. In the evening peace and quiet, the atmosphere over the park-like setting of the Việt-Nam Veterans Memorial felt even more solemn and soul-stirring.

Ready to head back to the hotel, I rose from the bench and moseyed on to the Wall to leave my token. Just then, I caught sight of a man dashing in from the southwest corner, where the bronze sculpture "The Three Soldiers" emerged from the shady trees. He appeared to be racing against the falling darkness but seemed utterly at a loss as to how to proceed. Starting at the far end of the West Wall, he scurried frantically but rather cluelessly from one panel to the next, his eyes skipping up and down the

columns of names on the glossy black granite without showing any signs of recognition. It was obvious he wasn't having success in his blind search.

I took a stroll in his direction, and we crossed each other near the apex, where the East and West Walls came together, just as banks of ground floodlights switched on and illuminated the entire monument like a stage.

"Need help locating your name, son?" I asked.

The man looked to be in his early thirties, tall and husky, with reddish-blond hair and a boyish, engaging grin. His handsome face was stubbly, with a five o'clock shadow, and shone with sweat and eagerness.

"Yes, sir. I'm trying to find Pa." He slipped his thick fingers through his crew cut and cast an uncertain glance around the park, deserted at this late hour. "But with all them names here … how d'you know where to start?"

"It might be easier to look in the daytime, even with the crowds."

"I was hoping to scout things out first before I bring my wife and my two boys here in the morning. Save some time, you know, seeing as how we only have a few days here." His sky-blue eyes crinkled up around the corners. "We arrived late this morning. The boys couldn't wait any longer, so we all went and had a long fun day at the Air and Space Museum. Mom and kids are all worn out and taking a nap at the hotel now."

I smiled, held out my hand. "I'm Roger, from California."

His grip was powerful yet friendly. "Nice to meet you, sir. My name's Eric, and we're from Minnesota. It's our first visit to the capital." He motioned with his head toward the shiny expanse of black wall. "I've always wanted to come and search for Pa's name up here."

"Ah, but there's a method to this seeming madness, you see. The names are inscribed in ascending chronological order, starting from right here on the East Wall and extending to its very end, then wrapping around the terrace to the far end of the West Wall, before coming full circle back to the apex here. It's meant to symbolize a wound that is closed and healing. So I've read."

Eric's eyes followed my sweeping hand around the plaza, taking it all in.

"Normally, the first thing you'd do is look up the name in the directories on those podiums over there to determine which panel it's on. But if you know the date your pa died, maybe I can save you time and point you to the right panel, or somewhere close to it at least."

He blinked, cleared his throat before answering. "It's January 14, 1968."

I jumped. "What a coincidence. That also happens to be the date for my hooch mate. I know exactly which panel it is, right in the middle of this East Wall—"

My breath suddenly caught in my throat. I did a double-take, staring speechlessly at the young man's expectant face. A sense of déjà vu registered at last, although I knew for a fact that we had never crossed paths before....

And then the light bulb came on.

But of course!

Eric—Eric the Red.

Little Ricky.

A shudder ran up my back. Could it *really* be?

Over the furious thumping in my temples, I heard myself stammering breathlessly:

"What—what's your pa's name, son?"

"Bob Olsen, sir."

My heart stopped. I gulped, heaved a big exhale through my dry mouth to try and relieve the vice-like tightness around my chest.

"Well, I'll be damned," I finally managed, shaking my head and smiling incredulously at the young man in front of me. "This is absolutely mind-blowing. Eric Olsen. Who would have guessed?" As he stared at me, bewildered, I reached over, gripped him by the shoulders, and gave him a vigorous shake. Breathing hard and fast, I heard the words tumble out of my mouth—a broken dam. "How in the world are you, son? I can't believe it's you. Of course, you don't know me at all; we've only just met. But I know—I've known—about you. My name is Roger Connors. Your pa and I were hooch mates in Việt-Nam during the war. And best buddies, too. Such a good man, he was. In fact, I came here early this afternoon to pay my respects—"

Catching the stunned expression on his face, I laughed and got a grip on myself.

"Come on, Eric. Let me just take you to your pa now. We'll have time to fill you in on all the details afterward."

It was another lifetime.

It was another country.

Summer 1967.

Having just finished my medical internship, I was commissioned into the USAF, with whom I had previously signed up in exchange for a deferment. With close to a half-million U.S. troops in combat in South Việt-Nam, there was a severe shortage of medical personnel to care for them, hence the "Doctor Draft." I was promptly shipped overseas to Biên-Hòa Air Force Base on the outskirts of the capital Sài-Gòn, where I was to serve a one-year tour as General Medical Officer. At the time the largest and most important logistical port in South Việt-Nam, Biên-Hòa also had the distinction of being the busiest airport in the world, military or civilian, bar none.

Sharing an 8'x20' two-men hooch at the base with me was a real Sky Doc—a USAF flight surgeon—a couple of years older than me, by the name of Bob Olsen. He was a tall, large-boned Minnesotan from the town of Little Falls, who more resembled a Green Bay Packers' lineman than a doctor, and a gentleman through and through. If not for him kindly taking me under his wing and showing me the ropes—from the minutiae of life in country to combat casualty care—there's no telling how disastrous the year might have turned out for me, a wide-eyed newbie who had never set foot outside California.

Over the months, as together we muddled through the war experience, we bonded and grew to be more than hooch mates— friends. I got to know Bob well and became aware of the two great passions in his life: his wife Nancy, the high school sweet-heart whom he had married right after med school, and pregnant with their first child before he had left for Việt-Nam; and aviation, a lifelong dream inspired by his hometown hero, Charles Lindbergh, the famous pioneer. A handmade sign tacked on the wall behind Bob's desk at the dispensary said it all, with this quote from an unknown source: "To most people, the sky is a limit. To those who love aviation, the sky is home."

This latter interest, however keen, was soon relegated to a distant third place after Nancy gave birth to their baby, just two weeks before Christmas.

Bob received the news via a surprise phone call from Minnesota, from Nancy herself. Prior to the big event, and without his knowledge, she and the family had arranged with Senator Barry Goldwater's ham radio shack in Paradise, Arizona, call sign AFA7UGA, for a special favor. It had been agreed that once the baby arrived, she could call in to the radio operators in Paradise; they would then use short-wave carriers to patch her phone line to the one in the dispensary at Biên-Hòa so she could talk with her husband. And so, after a twelve-hour labor, Nancy placed the call. When she finally got through and broke the happy news to Bob, it bowled him over, causing a big commotion in the back office where he was taking the call.

"It's a boy," roared the proud new papa as he rushed out from the office minutes later, his arms raised above his head in a triumphant touchdown signal. "Twenty-one inches, nine pounds eight ounces, with a set of lungs and an appetite to match!" Flushed with excitement, he dashed around the dispensary to pass out Muriel Magnum cigars to the staff. "Big surprise is, the little guy turns out to be a carrot top although we're all blond in our families. Nancy doesn't quite know what to make of it, but I rather think it's cute. My best Christmas gift—ever!"

"Y'all picked out a name yet?" shouted someone over the ruckus.

"Ricky, short for Eric. Eric Alexander Olsen."

"How fitting. A hearty welcome to Eric the Red, everyone," came the quick repartee amid wild cheers and applause.

Later, a small group of us took Bob to the Officers Club to celebrate, where he handed out more cigars, this time to his pilot friends. They back-slapped and toasted him uproariously, and some even gave him their pilot scarves—different colors from the different squadrons—right off their necks. "Special gifts for little Ricky from the flyboys," he proudly said upon returning from his victory lap, as he showed off the collection of scarves draped over his forearm.

In those dog days of war, all service people in Việt-Nam looked with great anticipation to the halfway point in our tour. It was when we were to be granted a week of Rest and Recreation at an out-country destination of our choice, from a designated list that included Thailand, Hong Kong, Japan, Australia, and Hawaii. For married personnel, special arrangements could also be requested for their spouses to join them during their R&R. Shortly after the birth of his son, Bob approached me to ask if I would mind swapping vacation schedules with him so that he could put in for a one-week leave in January and meet up with Nancy in Honolulu. Due to a thin staff, it was paramount that we coordinate our times off to ensure adequate coverage at the dispensary with minimal disruption.

"Be glad to, old man. It's no trouble at all," I said, and reminded him with a wink, "Hey, don't sweat the small stuff, Papa. You've got much bigger worries now."

Later that same week, a colleague of ours, Army doctor Dean Hunter, also a member of our close-knit circle on base, flew off to Hong Kong on his own R&R. Before he left, I asked him to pick me up a Chinese stuffed-toy dragon, in crimson preferably, while he was there.

"Whatever floats your boat, man," he deadpanned, hardly batting an eye.

"Not for me, you jackass," I clarified with a laugh. "It's for old man Bob to take with him to Hawaii next month, for his baby boy at home. Puff, the Magic Dragon? Got it? Bob is into it big time, but you know that. He'll get a real kick out of this. Trust me."

Puff was the nickname of the fabulous AC-47 gunship, call sign Spooky, a legend among U.S. servicemen in country and a terror for the Việt-Cộng on the battlefield. Basically a World War II Skytrain transport made over on-site at Biên-Hòa AFB, it was equipped to deliver crippling gun power. At nighttime, this had the visual effect of a cone of fire pouring down from the sky over the enemy. The dragon moniker, borrowed from the title of a popular folk song by Peter, Paul and Mary, was first coined by a reporter from the *Stars and Stripes* who had witnessed, in total awe, the gunship in action. As a proud member of the USAF and a huge fan of the folk-singing trio, Bob was completely taken with the newborn legend and with the song itself, whose catchy lyrics had been adapted by the AC-47 crews to better suit their story of war. So much so that I once teased him and asked if he might possibly consider naming a son of his "Puff." That had him in stitches, though he never did give a categorical negative.

His fondness for the song blossomed into a full-blown obsession after the birth of Ricky. Every evening before lights-out, Bob would play the record over and over on his RCA tabletop and bellow along without tiring. I finally understood why when one night, out of the blue, he interrupted his singing midstream and remarked, "This is a real cute children's song, isn't it, Roge? Like a sing-along fairy tale. I told Nancy it would make a sweet lullaby when the baby fusses at night." He then laughed and took a lighthearted jab at himself, "Ya, sure. Just not the way Papa butchers it, though. I'd scare the poor kid awake for good."

The Saturday before Bob was to fly to Hawaii, I had business to attend to in Sài-Gòn and missed the weekly excursion with the MEDCAP (Medical Civic Action Program) team. This was a rotating group of on-base volunteers who ventured into the countryside on the weekend to provide aid, medical and otherwise, to the local indigent. It happened to be Dollars-for-Scholars Weekend, and the team was scheduled to make the rounds of the classrooms in nearby villages. At each stop, they would present scholarships to outstanding students and pass out gifts of school supplies to the rest, before wrapping up with a vaccination clinic for all. Everyone on the team had been eagerly awaiting this special occasion and what promised to be a fun-filled, event-packed outing—the culmination of months of fundraising and planning.

Aside from me, Bob also had to miss that weekend's jaunt in order to run some errands at the BX and finish packing for his trip the next day. I had planned to wait until I returned on base that evening to give him his send-off surprise: the toy dragon that Dean Hunter had brought me back from Hong Kong. Bob's reaction when I revealed to him the meaning behind the stuffed toy would undoubtedly be priceless—the kind of stuff we hooch mates would reminisce and laugh about for years to come. The mere thought of it kept me chuckling all that day.

But as fate would have it, the surprise would be on me.

Earlier that morning, Capt. Silverman of the base Dental Corps, our Civic Action leader, had woken up with a virulent case of FUO (Fever of Unknown Origin): fever, shakes, nausea, diarrhea, the whole nine yards. To his dismay, he had no choice but to scrap his plans for the day and remain in bed. That meant the already shorthanded MEDCAP team would now be missing nearly half of its eight members. A cancellation and reschedule of the event appeared inevitable. There was just one problem, though, a rather significant one.

There had been such built-up anticipation on the part of the local schoolteachers and their young pupils that a last-minute postponement would surely cause huge disappointment. For the deprived children, who had so looked forward to receiving their gifts, the affair was to also mark their early celebration of Tết, the Vietnamese Lunar New Year, before school let out. No one had the heart to deny the kids that simple joy, if it could be helped.

Had I gotten wind of the breaking crisis before my departure for Sài-Gòn that morning, I certainly could—and would—have rearranged my plans in order to stay and sub-in for Capt. Silverman. As it happened, I would only learn about the turn of events and all its consequences much later. And so, in the end, it was Bob, a founding member of the Dollars-for-Scholars Committee, who stepped up and saved the day. According to the dispensary staff, when he was briefed about the situation, Bob simply said, in his unassuming, matter-of-fact way, "No sweat. I'll go with and give the guys a hand." He maintained he wasn't putting himself out in any way, for he was just about done packing for the trip. "But we've got to haul ass to make up for lost time," were his final words.

So off they went without further delay, carrying hefty bags of gifts aboard a Huey chopper nicknamed Patches. The affectionate moniker was meant as a badge of honor for the numerous pockmarks scored on its body by Charlie's gunfire.

On that weekend, however, Patches' legendary luck finally ran out.

While gliding above the palm trees along the Đồng-Nai River, the helicopter was raked by anti-aircraft fire from the jungles below. It plummeted from the sky only minutes after takeoff, exploding on the riverbank upon impact. According to stunned eyewitnesses on the ground, the scene was strewn with blood-stained debris and school supplies. Of the crew of four and the six passengers, not a single survivor. Search and Rescue was at once dispatched from the base and spent the rest of the day scouring proximate rice paddies for their scattered remains.

The news hit me like a shockwave upon my return to Biên-Hòa that night. I stumbled back to our hooch as Graves Registration Service was collecting and packing up all of Bob's personal effects to ship home. Within minutes, all traces of him had been cleaned out, leaving his side of the hooch eerily empty, as though it had never been occupied. In the hazy days that followed, I remained in utter shock and disbelief, barely going through the motions. With my best friend and mentor so suddenly yanked from my life, I found myself cast adrift without bearings. A hollow, unsettled feeling—as if a part of me had gone AWOL—would dog me for the rest of my tour.

No less disturbing were the questions that haunted my nights, the answers to which I never screwed up the courage to find out. Had the children and their teachers been forgotten and left waiting in the schoolyards for the gift bearers who never showed? Had someone on base been able to contact Nancy before she left for Hawaii? Dear God. Please let there have been family or friends by her side when some perfect stranger called with the news. Not all alone, stranded at an airport far away from home—or worse, waiting and wondering in a lonely honeymoon suite on Waikiki Beach. And then, of course, lurking in the back of my mind like a guilty secret, the most glaring question of all, the elephant in the room: Why him? Why Bob, who had so much to live for, and not *me*? Try as I might, I simply couldn't stop replaying the things Bob had shared with me earlier, all his plans and dreams for his family after he returned home.

But there was little time for questions—or grieving.

The tragedy served as an omen for darker times ahead. Two weeks after the fatal incident, all hell broke loose. The Việt-Cộng launched their Tết Offensive in blatant violation of the Lunar New Year's ceasefire, spreading death and destruction across South Việt-Nam on a scale never seen before. Biên-Hòa AFB itself was under withering attack and sustained rocket shelling almost nightly, earning it the notorious nickname "Rocket Alley." The hostilities had definitely moved into full gear. Life in country, as I had experienced it under Bob's guidance during my first six months, would not be the same again.

As the war raged on, sucking all of us into its deadly orbit from which many did not escape, I somehow managed to conclude my one-year tour physically unharmed. In July 1968, I boarded a Freedom Bird flight home, with the token memento of my service time in Việt-Nam, Puff the stuffed-toy dragon, tucked away at the bottom of my trunk.

As the Boeing 707 swept into the air, I stared out the window and watched the earth tumble away in a dizzying flash of colors: the deep-red soil of Biên-Hòa; the luxuriant shades of green from the triple-canopy jungle surrounding the base; the mirror ponds from a checkerboard of rice paddies; and, slithering eastward toward the blue Pacific, the silver snake of the Đồng-Nai River. A peaceful and striking tableau from above, shimmering like a treacherous mirage. Shortly after the plane had climbed through the upper layer of monsoon clouds, the cheerful pilot came on the PA to announce that we had reached altitude and were now safe and secure beyond the reach of anti-aircraft artillery. The cabin erupted in huge cheers and applause.

It hit me right then, smack between the eyes.

Bob should have been the one on this Freedom Bird, cheering and tossing his flight cap in the air in celebration with all the fellows.

I was the marked one, the one supposed to have gone up in the doomed chopper that day.

For years after coming home, I kept feeling like I had no business being here—breathing, walking, talking. Going to work. Getting married. Leading a "normal" life as though that were the natural order of things, unfolding in good time as preordained. In my gut, however, I knew better. It was all a cheat. A total freak of fortune.

I never attempted to look up Nancy Olsen and her baby. Nor did I talk about them or Bob—or much of my experience in Việt-Nam, for that matter—with my wife, Debbie. It wouldn't have changed any of our realities or made them better, and it might even have raised more of those troubling questions with no answers. Why open the Pandora's Box and let loose those harrowing memories of war and death on others, when no good could come of it? The best thing to do, I decided, was to keep that turbulent part of my past locked away deep inside, and just move on. Even in my foggy state of mind, I knew we all needed to—Debbie, Bob's family, me.

And moved on I had, over the decades. Or so I had thought.

And here we were. July 1998.

Thirty years flown by like the afternoon shadows that sweep across a lawn.

Call it a twist of irony. Or fate, once more. The Vietnamese have an intriguing name for it that stuck in my mind: *Con Tạo*, they call it, which translates literally as "Child Providence." A capricious child at play, with us mortals its playthings.

I had been sent by the hospital where I worked to attend a weeklong conference at Johns Hopkins University in Baltimore. At the last moment before leaving home, I had decided to pack

Puff the toy dragon in my suitcase. It was going to be my token, to be left with Bob—at the Wall under his name, where it really belonged. I had been carrying it around with me much too long.

And so, on this brilliant afternoon of my last day before flying home, I rode the train into the capital and paid my first visit to the Việt-Nam Veterans Memorial.

I led Eric to the proper panel in the middle of the East Wall and pointed out Bob's name on the black granite. He gazed at it, speechless, his eyes wide and glistening with emotion.

"I'd love to talk to you about your pa, when you're done here," I said softly. "But take your time, son. I'll just go sit and rest my old back on the bench over there." Waving Puff in my hand, I added, "You can't possibly know it, but this little bugger here actually belongs to you. I'll tell you a story about it later, and then you can take it with you when you go."

Standing next to me at the Wall, with a shaky smile on his lips, Eric nodded in silence. Then he raised his hand and, hesitantly and with reverence, touched the mirror-like black stone—the engraved name of his deceased father, with our merged reflections cast upon it. Slowly and thoughtfully, he let his fingers trace the finely etched letters.

I ambled to the bench and dropped down on it, suddenly feeling the weight of the years on my neck and shoulders. "Imagine that, old man," I whispered to my hooch mate, picking up the conversation I'd been having with him all day long. "Your boy

Ricky, a grown man and a father now. And you, a *grandpa*. When did this all happen? It seems like just yesterday you were running around, passing out cigars." Closing my eyes and exhaling deeply, I leaned against the hard backrest and surrendered to the sounds and images that had come flooding back all afternoon.

I saw Bob, even more fresh-faced and younger-looking than his son Eric now, pacing the dirt floor in our hooch in the deepening twilight of the tropics. He was belting out the song lyrics along with Peter, Paul, and Mary, tapping his feet to the rhythm while struggling to stay on key, as he imagined himself cradling his newborn son in his arms and singing him to sleep. The son he had never got to hold and had only known through pictures from home.

And I found myself smiling, then joining in, nodding and softly humming along with my hooch mate, as my lips registered the warm and salty taste of tears.

> *"Puff, the magic dragon, lived by the sea*
> *And frolicked in the autumn mist*
> *in a land called Honah Lee ..."*

Like a wound that is closed and healing, the little red dragon from the far-away land was finally coming full circle to its intended home—after three long decades.

And that, to me, was nothing short of magic.

Flowers in the Sky

Sài-Gòn, South Việt-Nam, September 1972

B inh had been looking forward all day to this evening. The boy, a skinny six-year-old with a pointed face and alert eyes under a mop of untamed black hair, was helplessly trying to sit still through dinner. Every few minutes, he would spring up from his chair and trot to the front door where his prized possession hung from the knob and gingerly touch it, as though afraid it might evaporate into thin air at any moment.

"Look, Má. Look!" he called back to his mother at the table. "*Máy bay đẹp quá*—isn't it the most awesome airplane you have ever seen?"

The object of his adulation was a toy lantern built from a frame of bamboo sticks covered with glossy, transparent red paper and shaped like a prop airplane. A short spiral wire affixed

to the bottom bar held a candle that could be lit to illuminate the lantern from inside. Looping over its wing tops was a string that suspended the airplane from a handle stick. The shiny toy had cost Bình every *xu* of his *tiền lì-xì*—the "lucky money" his parents and relatives had given him months earlier on the occasion of Tết, the traditional Vietnamese New Year holiday.

Má, a petite woman in her thirties with long black hair rolled up in a casual bun behind her neck, concurred with a smile. "*Đẹp lắm rồi*—yes, it is very pretty. Now get back here and finish eating."

As Bình scurried back to his seat and picked up his bowl and chopsticks, sweeping the rice into his mouth and swallowing it with hardly a chew, she went on, "We may be lucky after all. It doesn't look like it's going to rain. You kids will enjoy a beautiful *Trung-Thu* moon tonight."

Má was referring to the Mid-Autumn Moon that occurs on the fifteenth of the eighth month of the lunar calendar year, which usually falls around September. Also known as the harvest moon, it is considered the loveliest full moon of the year and is traditionally celebrated with the Mid-Autumn Festival, a popular holiday for children who go out parading their colorful lanterns after sunset then come home to feast on tasty mooncakes. In peaceful times, there may even be *múa lân*, the spirited Lion Dance, to lead off the parade. But September is still monsoon season in Sài-Gòn, and it is not unusual for the tropical showers to disrupt the festivities.

But not tonight, according to Má, and seldom was she wrong about anything. Bình was thrilled to hear that because he was itching to show off his new toy to the other children in their neighborhood, an overcrowded suburb on the outskirts of the city. In years past, he had gone to the Trung-Thu parade carrying old folded paper lanterns, the inexpensive type that opened up like small accordions. But after last year's festival, when he had been mercilessly taunted all evening for his "baby's toy," Bình had promised himself he would return this year with a real lantern, one worthy of a grown boy, for he surely saw himself as such.

Having kept an eye out for the perfect find since early in the month, he hadn't seen anything that had captured his attention— until a recent trip to the market with Má. As they sauntered past a small shop packed to its rafters with all kinds of fascinating knickknacks, Bình's eyes popped at the sight of an airplane in slick red paper dangling from the cobwebbed ceiling. This, his skipping heart shouted to him as he stood gazing with open mouth, was *exactly* what he wanted. The boy yanked on his mother's hand and begged her to stop in to check the price for him. Then as soon as they returned home, he rushed in and lugged his piggy bank out onto the kitchen table where he noisily spilled its contents on top of all the red envelopes of "lucky money" from Tết.

Huffing with excitement, he ran to drag Má by the hand to his pile of treasure. "Má *ơi*, can you help me count the money to see if there is enough here for the airplane?" he said.

With Bình kneeling on the chair next to her and watching with bated breath, Má started to count slowly so he could follow along with her, "Ten *xu*, fifty *xu*, two *đồng* . . ." Together they reached the final tally, with the boy yelling out: "Fifty-one *đồng* and twenty *xu!*"

Bình sank down in the chair like a deflated balloon. It was the most money he had ever had, but it still fell short of the asking price of seventy *đồng*, by a hopeless amount as far as he could figure. Despite his young age, he was aware that lately money had been tight around the house. Má had had to cut back on everything other than rice and fish sauce, so he kept mum about his disappointment and tried his hardest to be a grown boy about it.

But Má knew. She gave Bình a gentle squeeze on the shoulder. "Let me talk to the shop owner the next time I go to the market. Maybe he can come down in price a little."

If need be, Má thought, there was that money she had set aside to buy herself a new *nón lá*, the conical palm-leaf hat that Vietnamese women wear to shield their faces from the scorching sun or pelting rain. The one she owned had started to fray at the seams, but with care and a bit of luck, it might last her just a while longer, perhaps even until the end of the monsoon season.

So Má did what she needed to do and had returned from the market this afternoon with a small bag of vegetables in one hand and the airplane lantern in the other. Some neighbor kids playing outdoors dropped their kick-shuttlecock and scampered noisily after her. They reached out their little hands to try to touch the glossy red toy, and she had to keep raising it higher and away from them. When at last she crossed the doorway with the glistening trophy held at chest height in front of her, Bình bounded out to greet her with the loudest shriek she had ever heard from him. *It certainly seems true, what people say, that children blossom from moments like this,* Má told herself, chuckling at the euphoric expression on her boy's face.

Such happy moments, unfortunately, had been scarce in this Year of the Rat (1972), especially since early April. War, having smoldered for some time like ashes from an exhausted wildfire, had suddenly gathered fresh strength to rage anew all across the country, wreaking even more devastation than the Tết Offensive four years earlier. As the U.S. continued to press on with the withdrawal of its ground troops from Việt-Nam, the Communists from the North had seized the opportunity and launched their all-out Easter Offensive against the South Vietnamese people and army. The death toll mounted and locale after locale was reduced to smoking rubble as the fierce fighting escalated into the Summer of Red Fire. Once again, Má was tossing and turning late into the night to the ominous rumbles in the distance, praying with all her might for the safety of her husband, Bình's father.

As members of the elite Airborne Forces in the South Vietnamese Army, he and his fellow paratroopers were continually mobilized from one hot spot to the next, sometimes vanishing for months on end at a moment's notice. Every time his letters home, scribbled in haste and smeared with mud, sweat, and gunpowder, were interrupted for more than a couple of weeks, Má could only surmise that her husband and his soldier brothers had been embroiled in knock-down, drag-out combat on some unnamed battlefield in no man's land.

To spare Bình and his grandparents constant worry, Má bore the burden of anxiety in silence and prayed to the ancestors to protect her husband and return him home safely to them. Her long black hair that he adored had started streaking gray in recent months. On his last forty-eight-hour leave early this summer, in a rare interlude of romantic escape, he had surprised her with a bright red bloom of *phượng-vỹ* from the majestic poinciana trees that shaded the streets of Sài-Gòn. Tucking it in her hair as he used to do back when they had been students at the university, he had spotted the new gray strands, and without a word, had pulled her into his arms and held her tight. Ten years had flown by since those wide-eyed university days, and it was plain that war and the hard life had caught up to them. In that bittersweet moment, her head resting on his shoulder, together they had mourned the last of younger, more innocent times.

That was why Má had vowed to do whatever she could to keep her only child from having to grow up too fast. She did not mind the personal sacrifices that such an endeavor imposed, for in exchange it gave her a sense of control, however minute and fragile, over their lives.

Swallowing the last mouthful of rice, Bình set down his bowl and chopsticks and propped his elbows on the table, his small face in his hands. "I wish Ba could see my new airplane," he said, clicking his tongue in regret. "Do you think he will like it, Má?"

"Just wait until your father sees it the next time he gets home," Má answered in a bright tone, despite not knowing when that might actually be. "He will absolutely love it, there's no doubt about that. In fact, it looks just like the real ones he and his friends jump out of."

Bình grinned broadly. He had chosen this lantern thinking of Ba, missing him and yearning to feel close to him. Every time Ba came home, which lately had been rarely, Bình would beg to don his helmet, its lining and strap mottled with dried sweat and smelling of battlefields. Though it was several sizes too big for him and almost covered his eyes completely, the boy was thrilled to feel the weight of it on his head. Thus protected with his father's steel hat, he would climb up on a chair then jump off to the ground while loudly firing an imaginary gun, *tak-tak-tak*. Over and over again, he would dash through the same motion, a little faster each time, never tiring of the simple game.

Watching him play, Ba had once remarked, "You sure make a good little 'trooper, son."

As Bình beamed with pride, Ba set down the large boots he was polishing and motioned to the boy to come sit by him on the floor. Helmet askew and cheeks flushed from all the jumping, Bình plopped down next to his father, his little legs folded in the same seated position.

"When I grow up," he said in a rush of breath, "I want to be a good soldier like you, Ba."

His father reached over and rubbed the top of the steel hat. "You will defend me and Má against the bad guys, right? Because I'm going to be a tired old man by then, you know."

"I will protect you and Má," Bình said solemnly, peering out from under the helmet.

"Fighting is always messy," Ba continued. "Someone is bound to get hurt. When you're at school, I want you to try and stay out of trouble as much as you can. But trouble has a way of finding you, no matter your good intentions. Like if some big, mean boys keep picking on you for no reason and just won't leave you alone, then you have got no choice but to stand up for yourself. Right, son?"

"Yes, Ba. I will stand up for myself," Bình said, sitting up a little taller.

His father nodded pensively before going on, "It takes courage and sacrifices to stand up for oneself—and for others, too. Do you know what people sometimes call us paratroopers?"

The boy shook his head, knocking the oversized helmet further off-kilter.

"*Thiên thần mũ đỏ,*" Ba said with a wistful smile. "Angels in red berets. Not because we have any kind of divine power. Far from it. But what's true is wherever there are helpless people in danger from the Việt-Cộng, we risk our lives and jump down from the sky to rescue them."

Bình waited a moment then asked, "Ba *ơi,* where is your beret now?"

"We only wear it on special occasions," Ba said, springing to his feet. "Wait here. I will be right back with it."

When his father returned with the crimson-colored felt hat that smelled faintly of mothballs, the young boy struggled out of the heavy helmet, set it squarely on his lap, then reached up with both hands. "May I hold it? Please?"

The red beret looked striking with a black leather headband, a narrow black ribbon sticking out the back, and an embroidered badge toward the front depicting a white parachute encircled by a pair of golden wings. A small yellow flag with three red stripes, the South Vietnamese flag, was stitched to the bottom of the badge where the two wings joined.

Bình pressed the beret to his face and took a deep breath. "Mmm. It feels so nice," he said, his voice muffled through the soft fabric.

Peeling the felt hat from his face, the boy examined the embroidery with awed curiosity as his fingers ran back and forth over the white parachute. "What is it like, Ba? Up there."

His father dropped back on the floor next to him. "When we jump, we just concentrate on landing quickly and safely, so there's not much time to think about anything else," he said. "But even so, I can tell you there is no feeling in the world quite like it— gliding through the air weightless-like, just the sound of silence except for the wind whistling in your ears." Ba paused, his eyes slightly squinting, then continued in a softer voice, "It's a beautiful sight when all the 'chutes open up one after another. Just like new blossoms popping out, up there in the open sky. That is why folks often call them *hoa dù*—parachute flowers." Clearing his throat, he ruffled up Bình's hair with his hand. "Tell you what, son. Next year, I will try to make it home to take you and Má to the big parade on Armed Forces Day. You will see what I mean."

"Really, Ba? Really?" the young boy cried, jumping and waving the red beret over his head. How awesome it would be, he thought, to turn his face up to the sky and watch dozens of those *hoa dù* blossom in bright sunlight, then see them catch the wind and float down gracefully to earth. Most important, though, Ba would be there to point things out every step of the way and share in the excitement with him and Má. It would be the greatest treat of all: a fun outing with the whole family together. The boy could hardly contain himself.

Ba smiled. "I hope by the time you grow up there won't be any more fighting, and we can go parachuting just for fun. Má and I want that for you more than anything. It's the reason we chose to name you Bình, as in *hoà-bình*—peace." He lowered his head to catch the boy's eyes. "Have you any idea what you want to be when you're all grown up—besides a 'trooper, of course?"

Bình wrinkled his nose. "A pilot?" he ventured after some thought. "Then I can fly *any* airplane I want. But can I be a doctor, too? They help wounded people and soldiers."

Ba draped his arm around Bình's shoulders, pulling the boy close to him. "You have a kind heart, that's a good place to start. Now behave yourself in school, study hard, and fill that bright head of yours with knowledge, and you can achieve anything, son."

"Ba ơi, what did *you* want to be when you grew up?"

Caught off guard, Ba blew out a long breath before answering. "Me? I had always wanted to follow in the footsteps of *Ông Nội*— Grandpa—and become a schoolteacher. I love books, and I like to teach them to curious young kids like you. But for now . . ."

"For now, you are an angel in a red beret," Bình finished his sentence, and Ba cracked up as the boy tried on the oversized hat and it slipped down past his nose.

Such moments spent with Ba were rare and much too short, and Bình never knew when he might see him next. Today, all day, the boy had been hoping that at any minute his father would burst in through that door and surprise him and Má with his unannounced day-leave. What a thrill it would be to show Ba his treasured new toy and to listen to him tell more stories of airplanes and parachutes, stories that Bình would eagerly share with his friends at the parade of lanterns later on. But it sure looked like that was not going to happen now. Not tonight.

Má got up from the table and began clearing the dirty bowls and plates. "Are you going to stop by Tiến's house first?" she asked. Tiến was Bình's best friend in the neighborhood, and the two boys had just started school together in the same first-grade class.

"I promised to go to the parade with him and his little sister," Bình said. "And then we will go back to their place and eat mooncakes."

"In that case, I am packing a couple of *bánh dẻo* for you to take and share with them."

She placed the goodies in a colorful cardboard box. They were snowskin mooncakes made of glutinous white rice flour with mung bean filling, and fragrant with the sweet banana oil that made Bình's mouth water. One was a traditional square, decorated with intricate floral imprints from the cake mold (Má had already set aside an extra square for Ba in the event he came home unexpectedly); the other was half as thick and shaped like a miniature roast pig, a popular design with children. The mooncakes had cost Má a good bit extra because they were only sold around this time of year, specifically for the Mid-Autumn Festival. But then, Má thought as she smiled at the ravenous twinkle in Bình's eyes, you're only a kid once.

She handed her son the precious parcel and patted him on the head. "Now grab your lantern, and don't forget the colored candles with it," she said. "Go have fun."

The boys lived just a short walk from each other in the same overcrowded district on the outskirts of Sài-Gòn. Bình took a dark and narrow alley that wound its way through a maze of low-cost dwellings covered with thatch or tin roofs and tightly jammed together. Tiến's house stood out in the night shadow, a rare two-story and one of a handful of houses that boasted a tile roof. As an additional sign of distinction, it was fronted by a small cement courtyard separated from the public walkway by a picket fence. Tiến's father worked at the nearby USAID office—a coveted, well-paid job, in terms of local wages—and his family had been the first in the neighborhood to own a television, a sixteen-inch black-and-white Sanyo set with grainy pictures. For a while, before a few more TV sets began to turn up in other households, his courtyard had been swamped every evening with curious neighbors who streamed by to gawk at the wonder box through the bars in the front window.

Tiến was pacing around the small yard, his eyes peering anxiously over the picket fence. He dashed out in front of it the instant he saw his friend emerge from the dark alley.

"What took you so long? I was afraid something happened and you were not coming," he blurted, then caught sight of the airplane lantern in Bình's hand and stopped short, his mouth agape. "Where did you find *that*? Đẹp dễ sợ—it's awesome!"

Although the same age as Bình, Tiến was at least half a head taller and quite a bit stouter, with a happy face, big round eyes, and a close crew cut. Neighbor kids had nicknamed him Ông Địa after the fat, bald, and merry God of the Land, but that only made his smile even broader.

"I had to look a *real* long time before I found it," Bình explained with an air of importance while trying hard to not appear he was bragging. "There was only one like it in the whole market. Má said it looks just like the airplanes that carry Ba and his soldier friends." Then, pushing the box of mooncakes in Tiến's hand, "Here. She gave us these to eat after the parade."

Tiến took the box and scampered back into the yard, followed by his friend. "Let me run tell Thùy you are here," he said without turning and promptly disappeared into the house.

He returned in a flash, accompanied by a little girl about four or five years old with dimpled round cheeks and double ponytails tied up with rubber bands and colored beads. They were each holding a cellophane-paper lantern in their hands.

As soon as she saw Bình, Thùy flashed a big smile that revealed a couple of missing front teeth and trotted up to him. "Look, look at my lantern. You like?" she asked, thrusting it by the handle stick in Bình's face. "It's a yellow butterfly. I say it's prettier than that orange fish Big Brother has. What do you think?"

"Butterflies are for girls," her brother interrupted. "And mine is a magic carp like the one for the Kitchen God, not just any fish. I sure like it better than a rabbit or a star." He cast an envious glance at Bình's airplane. "But I like *yours* even more. I wish I had seen it first at the market."

"I like both of yours, too," Bình said in a conciliatory tone, feeling confident and generous in the knowledge that his lantern was the best by far. "And they will all look even more beautiful when they are lit." He stared up at the night sky, which had turned golden bright with scarcely a cloud. "The moon is up already. Are we going soon?"

Tiến peeked over the fence at the empty alley. "A few more kids are still coming. How about we light the candles while we're waiting for them? I'll call my mother to come help us."

He handed his fish lantern to Bình and scuttled back into the house. It wasn't long before he came running out ahead of a woman about the same age as Má, with a permed hairdo and dimpled round cheeks just like Thùy's.

"*Dạ chào Bác*—hello, Auntie," Bình said.

"Is that you, Bình?" Tiến's mother answered. "*Chèn ơi*—my, my. What a pretty lantern you have there!" Her words were music to Bình's ears, and the boy puffed up with pride.

The woman pulled out a box of matches. The children huddled around her to form a shield against the rising breeze, and with great care, she lit their lanterns one by one.

"Ồ, lookie here!" Thùy cried out, her eyes and mouth open wide and her face gleaming in the candlelight. "My butterfly! It's prettier than the moon."

Bình didn't utter a word—mesmerized by the warm, red glow from his own lantern. It was as if the flickering candle had breathed life into the airplane, and the boy could almost feel its engines shaking and roaring, ready to shoot flames and launch it into the night sky. Do Ba and his friends go riding in the belly of such a firebird every day? Bình wondered.

Tiến was standing still next to his friend, holding his lit magic carp, but his eyes were glued to the shimmering airplane. He clicked his tongue and mumbled once again, "It's awesome."

His mother smiled. "Yes, they *all* look awesome, all your lanterns," she said, giving her boy an affectionate pat on the back. "And you couldn't ask for better weather for the parade. Just be extra careful with the candles. All right, children? Now, go enjoy.

Bình's mother sent along some mooncakes, and I've a few of my own, too. There will be plenty to eat when you get back." She sauntered back to the house and left the children to themselves to celebrate their special night.

"Can anyone see the fairy Hằng-Nga?" Thùy asked, squinting up at the bright moon. "They say she is beautiful and she lives in a big castle up there. But I can't even see the castle."

Bình shook his head. "That's just a kids' fairytale. There was never any fairy on the moon," he explained to the little girl whom he treated as his own baby sister. "But I can clearly see Chú Cuội, the woodchopper. He flew up to the moon on his Magic Banyan Tree, you know."

Thùy stretched up on her tiptoes. "Where? Where?"

"See those dark shadows up there?" Bình waggled his finger at the golden disk. "Use your finger to trace them like so, and you can make out the tall banyan tree with its long branches. And that's Chú Cuội himself sitting at the foot of the tree, all alone and homesick for Earth."

Tiến arched his eyebrows. "I don't know about all that. My father said the Americans went to the moon and found nothing up there. Only rocks."

His sister turned to Bình, a finger on her chin. "Does your father's airplane fly as high as the moon? Maybe he can peek out the window and tell us what he sees."

Bình did not think the airplane could fly that high, but he felt certain Ba would be able to settle whether Tiến's father was right or not. However, the boy hoped with all his heart that Chú Cuội and the Banyan Tree wasn't just another tale. There was something truly magical about riding a big tree all the way to the moon, and he loved that story and wanted to keep believing it. "Good idea, Thùy. I'll remember to ask Ba the next time he gets home," he promised.

"Here come some others," Tiến shouted and rushed to throw open the fence gate.

A chirpy bunch of kids poured into the yard, each carrying a brightly lit lantern. Commotion ensued as the children fluttered around to compare and admire each other's prized possessions. Many swarmed around Bình, ogling his airplane and showering him with envious compliments, and the boy relished every minute of it. What a difference a year—and a proper lantern—made. In a little while, the whole group would file out the gate and follow the maze of narrow alleys all through the neighborhood—jostling, singing, laughing, as the Trung-Thu parade got underway and filled their world with light and wonder, albeit for one short night.

Someone grasped Bình's free hand and yanked on it. "Where have you been hiding?"

He swung around. His heart sank when he recognized Bà Tám Thợ May—Mrs. Eighth the Seamstress—whose name indicated both her livelihood and her order among her siblings. Bà Tám was old and short with a portly build, and she lived alone in a shack across the way from Má and Bình. The boy did not like her because she always yelled at him and the neighbor kids for making too much noise that interfered with her enjoying her favorite programs of *cải-lương* (classical Vietnamese opera) on the radio.

"You're wanted back at home," she said in her usual gruff voice. "Right away."

"Did Má say that? Because I just got here."

"Don't you argue with me," Bà Tám snapped. "I'm just sent to get you. It's all I know."

Tiến and Thùy witnessed the exchange from afar and scurried over.

"I have to stop back home for something," Bình told them with a puzzled scowl. "But I'll be back as soon as I can."

Thùy waved at him. "Don't be long. We won't eat the mooncakes until you're here."

On the way home, Bình had to hustle behind Bà Tám in order to keep up with her, his lantern swinging wildly with each hurried stride, casting bouncing pools of light on the ground. But his thoughts were racing even faster. What was so important that he had to be sent for immediately? Had Má gotten sick? Had she had an accident? Or maybe something had happened to Ông, Bà—his grandparents—who lived on the other side of town? Their health, already frail, had given Má new worries recently. Bình's steps suddenly got tangled up, and he almost tripped.

Huffing to catch up to his older neighbor, he called out to her, "Please wait up, Bà Tám. Why are you walking so fast? What is going on?"

Without missing a beat or looking at him, she grumbled, "Just hurry up and get home." But her voice sounded a bit softer, and she slowed down some.

They turned the last corner onto his block. It took a second or two before Bình realized there was a crowd gathered outside his house. Bright light in the front room spilled out into the dark alley, which was odd because Má always kept just one bulb on to save electricity. The boy's stomach clenched. Before another thought crossed his mind, his small feet had already taken off and propelled him past Bà Tám toward the house. The airplane bobbled precariously from the handle stick in his grip, its candle flittering like a lightning bug about to burn out.

Someone shouted his name. The crowd parted for him.

Bình shot through the open doorway.

"Má ơi, Má!" he yelled out, almost dizzy from his heart racing so fast.

And then he saw her—stretched out lifeless on the bamboo cot in the corner, with Auntie Mai leaning over her from a chair by the bedside. Bác Mai was a nurse and a family friend who lived down the block from them. Her children went to the same school as Bình.

The boy stopped cold. Not daring to breathe, he edged up to the bed.

Under the bright lamps, Má looked sickly pale, and her eyes were shut. Bác Mai was rubbing strong-smelling camphor oil on Má's temples and between her eyebrows. A couple of neighbors hovered around, massaging her arms and legs.

"Má *ơi*, Má!" Bình repeated softly, his voice shaking as tears welled up in his eyes.

Bác Mai looked up. Her forehead was dappled with sweat. "Ồ, good. Bà Tám found you," she whispered. "Your mother had a fainting spell, but thank heavens she didn't bump her head. She's still in shock, though. We should let her rest." Then with her chin she pointed behind him.

"Bình *à*," a familiar voice called out from behind.

The boy turned around. His eyes opened wide, then a relieved smile spread across his lips.

"Uncle Nam!" he said.

Chú Nam was one of Ba's closest paratrooper friends and had been to their house for dinner many times. Bình adored him because even though he was not very big or tall, he looked weathered, strong, and fierce—as a soldier should—and he always had a laugh-out-loud joke or thrilling combat story to share. But the best part about Chú Nam was, whenever he showed up at their doorstep, it meant Ba was coming home on leave also.

In his panic dash, Bình had completely missed him standing back by the table—bareheaded, his hair and face and his fatigues covered with red dust.

"Did you and Ba just get back?" Bình asked. "Does Má know you're here?" His gaze darted around the room, and his voice rose higher despite himself. "Where is Ba? Ba *ơi*, Ba!"

Chú Nam took a few steps toward him. "Bình *à* ..." he said again as he placed a hand on the boy's shoulder and reached out his other hand to gently take the lantern from him.

Bình jerked away, shielding the lantern with his body. There was something alarmingly strange about Chú Nam tonight—his tone of voice, the way he acted, that crooked grimace on his face. Bình stared up into his eyes. They were bloodshot with black circles under them as they always were each time he and Ba returned from the front, but absent from them now was that mischievous, winking smile that made you laugh whenever he came around. Instead, his eyes were glistening with such love, caring, and—sadness?—that it made Bình shiver all over.

"I want to show Ba my airplane," the boy said, his voice breaking.

Hot and icy fingers prickled the skin on his chest and back, then quickly spread to his entire body. Bình felt the shakes coming on, uncontrollable, like those times in the past when he had caught the flu. There was a buzzing in his ears that grew louder by the second, drowning out the *thump-thump-thump* of his heartbeat and Chú Nam's voice.

"I am so sorry, Bình ... last night ... jump mission ... your father ... shot down ..."

The lantern slipped out of Bình's hand and crashed to the floor.

A woman's voice shrieked as the boy watched, transfixed, his airplane go up in flames.

Suddenly he was falling through the sky, the air whistling past his ears. All around him were white parachutes—billowed up in the wind like blossomed flowers, but all on fire. It was blindingly bright, so hot and suffocating, as if the whole world were burning up. Even the clouds were singed a deep red, like the rims around Chú Nam's bloodshot eyes.

But Ba, Bình's angel in a red beret, was nowhere in sight.

The boy thought his chest was about to burst. Smoke and bitter tears stung his eyes.

"Ba *ơi*, Ba!" he cried, but not a sound escaped his parched throat.

And then—darkness swooped down over him. A sea of thick, black ink.

The last thing the boy felt was Chú Nam's strong arms catching him, breaking the fall.

San Jose, California, September 2002

The minivan swiftly pulled into the just vacated parking space, the driver chuckling happily over his lucky timing. At this late afternoon hour, finding parking anywhere, much less at this popular strip mall, was a challenge he had braced himself for. It was a common problem all over the crowded Bay Area, with harried nine-to-fivers rushing to the stores on their way home from work to grab last-minute items needed for family dinner.

He promptly parked, hopped out, and stepped around to the passenger side to pull open the sliding door. An Asian man of thirty-something dressed in business casual attire, he was slight of build and wore short-cropped hair and a weary look on his face despite the still lingering smile. It had been a hectic morning at the office, and the maddening rush-hour traffic on the highways here had done little to disperse the stress. Not to mention that his wife had stayed home sick today, and he had had to cut short his workday to run pick up their six-year-old boy at school before the daycare center closed. Unbuttoning his shirt collar under the loosened tie, the man reached inside the minivan and released the seatbelts that secured the booster seat. The little boy immediately clambered down from it. His father gave him his hand to lean on and helped him off the vehicle.

"Why are we stopping here?" the boy asked, even as his little sneakers touched the ground.

"Well, Mommy is sick, so you and I are responsible for dinner tonight," his father said. He slid the door closed behind them while holding on to the boy's hand. "We're stopping here to pick up the food. Anybody hungry for barbequed-pork fried rice and *chả giò*—egg rolls?"

"Yeah, barbequed pork and *chả giò*!" the boy cheered, kicking one foot high. "And fortune cookies, too. I'm *starved*!"

Rather small for his years, he had exuberant black hair that refused to lie flat and a baby face dominated by round glasses covering his inquisitive eyes. The spitting image of his father at the same age except for the glasses, his grandmother had always maintained. A bubbly boy, he was even more talkative this afternoon and had chattered nonstop the entire drive from school to the strip mall. It had been a great surprise for Daddy to pick him up, and he was eager to tell him about all the neat things he had learned in class today. There was a lot to tell, too, this being his first month in first grade. Each new day brought more exciting discoveries.

As they carefully crossed the busy parking lot toward the one Vietnamese restaurant in the mall, the boy yanked on his father's hand. "Daddy, can I go play with Tommy at his house this weekend? He asked me today."

"Who's Tommy?"

"I told you already. He's my new friend. He sits next to me in class."

"Does he live near us?"

"I don't know, but Mommy does. She is friends with his mom. They speak when she comes to pick me up at school." Then, remembering a detail that he felt might help his cause, the boy said, "And they talk in Vietnamese, like you and Mommy with Grandma."

Ah, another family of Vietnamese immigrants, the father noted with interest. There happened to be none in their immediate neighborhood, and it would be a good experience for the boy to finally have a playmate who shared the same cultural background.

He pushed the door, and they entered the small restaurant whose sparse decoration belied its popularity. Even though it was just past six o'clock, all the plain wooden chairs and tables in the noisy dining room were already occupied by a clientele predominantly Asian. The smells of pan-fried foods and spicy broths permeated the place, causing father and son's stomachs to growl.

They got in line at the busy cash register that also served as the reception counter.

"So can I go then, Daddy?" the boy pleaded, pulling again on his father's hand. "Please?"

"Is it Tommy's birthday or something?" the father asked, glancing distractedly at the frantic waiters rushing back and forth with steamy plates hoisted high in both hands.

"No, but he says there will be cakes and candles and lanterns . . ."

Somebody ahead of them had just finished, and they moved up in the queue. "I will talk it over with Mommy later, when she's feeling better. Okay?" the father said appeasingly.

When their turn came, the to-go order he had called in ahead was ready and waiting in a big brown bag behind the counter. With wordless efficiency, the busy clerk rang him up, accepted payment, and handed the bag over. The entire transaction took less than two minutes. They left, but instead of returning to their minivan, the father headed toward the Asian food market next door. "We'll make a real quick stop in here," he told the boy as he picked up a handbasket at the entrance, setting the bag of to-go food in it. "Mommy asked me to get a couple of things for her and some bananas for you to have with your cereal in the morning. We're all out of them."

It was one of those wonder shops, not especially large yet loaded with all kinds of goodies a Vietnamese housemaker would need to prepare an authentic traditional meal: from locally raised exotic produce and meats to imported rare spices and ingredients, to pre-cooked and ready-to-eat foods as well as a wide array of miscellaneous items commonly found in an Asian household.

The man made a beeline for the fruit and produce aisle, his young son trailing behind him.

"Daddy, look at all these neat boxes," the boy piped up as they strode by stacks of colorful cardboard boxes piled high on a long table in the middle of the central aisle. The decoration on their covers depicted a beautiful Asian woman in flowing ancient garb, with a golden full moon above her head. "What's in them? Who is that woman?"

"The pretty lady is the fairy Hằng-Nga, and those are boxes of *bánh Trung-Thu*, what else?" a passing friendly store clerk chimed in to answer the boy before his father could. "Real yummy, too, they are," he added with a wink before dashing away.

Glued to the floor in front of the colorful stacks, a finger poking at his chin, the boy leaned in for a better look. "What is *bánh Trung-Thu*, Daddy? Can we get a box of it?"

The father froze. Breathing a soft sigh, he closed his eyes momentarily.

Earlier on, he had spotted the boxes as he and his son were heading down the aisle, but it was too late to backtrack. All he could do was turn a blind eye to them. With all the busy doings at home and in the office, he had totally forgotten that this was the time of year when Vietnamese immigrants all across America, in homage to their heritage, would be celebrating Trung-Thu, the Mid-Autumn Festival. Nonetheless, he had hoped that his observant young son would not notice the boxes and start bombarding him with questions.

Not that the man had anything against traditions—far from it, thanks in no small part to his mother, the boy's grandma, who lived with them. But it so happened that this was one custom from the ancestral homeland that he didn't care to observe and had avoided altogether.

For thirty years now, since that tragic night in the fall of 1972, Bình had studiously banished any festive memory of Trung-Thu from his mind. No more moon cakes or candle-lit lanterns on that day again, even during the remaining years of his childhood. For him and his mother, the day had forever lost its traditional happy meaning and had become, instead, the anniversary of his father's death, a time for quiet sorrow and remembrance. Every year at Trung-Thu, they would arrange offerings of fresh fruit and flowers on the small altar that displayed the black-and-white photo of his father in full military uniform, complete with insignias and medals, shoulder cords, and beret—the same beret Bình had admired as a kid. Then he and Má would light a pair of red candles and three sticks of incense on the altar, bow their heads, and say a prayer for Ba. It was always a silent prayer from Bình, who even as a child had learned to keep quiet about his own distress over the events of that night for fear it might rekindle all the grief and pain for Má.

Now, slowly, he traipsed back to his son, who still stood mesmerized by the colorful boxes.

"They're called *bánh Trung-Thu,* or mooncakes," he began with hesitation, reaching his arm around the boy's back. "An old custom we have, to celebrate the full moon at this time of year."

"How come we never had them before? When is the full moon, Daddy?"

Bình cleared his throat before replying as casually as he could, "Soon. I think." But the first part of the kid's innocent question, to which he had no ready answer, had stirred up something inside him. All these years, his son had been deprived of this simple childhood pleasure because of what had happened on that night of Trung-Thu long ago—decades before the child had even been born. Suppressing a sigh, Bình pulled his son closer and gently tousled his hair.

The boy looked up, a glimmer of realization in his eyes. "Is that why Tommy asked me to come over this weekend? Because it's a special full moon?" His alert gaze suddenly zoomed past his father's shoulders, toward the ceiling behind them. His eyes now immense behind the round glasses and his mouth agape, he pointed excitedly. "Oh . . . Daddy. *Lookit. Look!*"

Bình whirled around. Hanging in the corner was a grouping of old-fashioned lanterns made of wooden sticks and painted fabric or cellophane paper of brilliant colors, quite similar to the kind that he had known and loved as a child. They were prominently on display, eye-catching props to remind busy shoppers of the upcoming festive occasion.

The boy broke away from his father, drawn toward the shiny objects like a bug to the light.

"Daddy," he shouted, reaching up with both hands. "There's an airplane up there! I want it."

A few steps behind his son, Bình stopped dead in his tracks.

Among the lanterns of various shapes and colors, a lone airplane coated in glossy red paper dangled gloriously from the end of its handle stick. At quick glance, it bore an eerie resemblance to the one he had bought with every *xu* in his piggy bank and a big sacrifice from Má, all those years ago on his doomed and final celebration of Trung-Thu.

And then, without warning, the floodgate gave way. Memories came rushing in, gray and blurry at first, then increasingly brighter and sharper as Bình's mind's eye continued to adjust. Images spilled forth in haphazard fashion, rolling and tumbling over each other to surge to the forefront: colored candles and mooncakes in the shape of miniature roast pigs; the triumphant look on Má's face when she strode through the door brandishing the airplane in her hand; the magical candlelight that breathed life into all the children's lanterns; the missing tooth and dimpled smile of Thùy, rising on tiptoes to stare at the moon in search of Hằng-Nga and Chú Cuội; the red rims and hollow circles around Chú Nam's eyes, bloodshot and haunting; beads of perspiration on Má's forehead as she lay deathly still on the cot; his prized airplane crashing to the floor, burning bright and hot like Ba's parachute. . . .

Bình's knees went weak under the surprise onslaught. He felt nauseous and lightheaded, as he had in that moment—so long ago, yet forever branded on his mind—when Chú Nam had sent him into shock with the devastating news. Leaning against the nearest counter, his shirt sticking like flypaper to his back, Bình took several quick breaths and a dry swallow, shook his head, and tried to blink away the avalanche of images.

A small hand slipped into his, and an anxious small voice asked, "Daddy, are you okay?"

Opening his eyes, he squeezed his son's hand and forced a smile. "Daddy's fine," he said in as bright a tone as he could muster. "Just a little hungry, is all." After a deep inhale, he picked up the basket again and nodded. "Now, let's just go get the stuff for Mommy, and then we can head home and enjoy all this yummy restaurant food."

The boy made no attempt to budge, however. He clung on to Bình's hand, swinging it back and forth as he always did before pleading for a favor. "Daddy, I *really, really* like that airplane. Can I . . . can I have it now . . . for my *next* birthday gift?" Then, his eager eyes wide with hope, he reminded Bình, "It's only two months away."

Still clutching his father's hand, the boy turned and craned his neck to gaze anew, with mixed deference and admiration, at the shiny red lantern. "Grandma says Grandpa and his soldier friends jumped out of airplanes all the time. Did they look like this one, Daddy?"

Bình felt the air knocked out of him, his upper body suddenly gripped in a vice.

"Grandma . . . Grandma said that to you? What else did she say?"

"She tells me stories about Grandpa when he was young—what a brave soldier he was," the boy babbled on. "But you don't want to talk about him because it makes you sad, she says."

His son's innocent words jolted Bình—a punch to the gut. He couldn't believe what he was hearing. For three decades now—practically his entire life since age six—he and Má had tiptoed on eggshells around each other, carrying their grief in stoic silence, because each of them had meant to spare the other the revisited trauma of that night. The result, ironically, had been the exact opposite. They had both suffered in secret while at the same time struggling on their own to keep Ba's memory alive any which way they could.

Poor Má. No wonder her hair had turned salt-and-pepper, and then salt, as far back as he could remember. What a crushing—and unnecessary—burden for her to shoulder all this time. He should know. He had been lugging around the same heavy load himself.

His chest swelling with emotion, Bình felt the sharp sting in his eyes and quickly turned his head. But not fast enough to escape the notice of his young son.

The boy hesitated a moment before touching his father's forearm and shaking it gently, a slight tremor in his voice. "Are you mad at me, Daddy? Because I talked about Grandpa?"

Still speechless, Bình managed to shake his head as he hugged the boy to his side.

Swallowing the lump in his throat, he answered at last, "No, I'm not mad at you. Not at all. But thanks for reminding me that I've got so much to tell you about Grandpa . . ."

. . . and airplanes and flowers in the sky—and a whole lot more, too. All those things that filled my heart and made me the man I am today. The ancestral homeland, half the world away, where Grandma and I and your mother came from; my early childhood years, deprived of material things but more than made up for with love and happiness; the horrors of war that robbed our family of Grandpa, and me as a child of my innocence; the terrifying escape to the ocean on a flimsy boat in the final hours of the war; our tentative first steps on this foreign soil as Grandma and I arrived in our adopted homeland, when I was just nine years old. . . .

But all in good time, when you're grown up enough to understand and care. As for now—

"What do you say we get you that airplane before someone else grabs it?" Bình said, draping an arm around his son's shoulders and leading him toward the coveted object.

The boy was hopping with joy. "Really, Daddy? You mean it?"

"Didn't you tell me earlier that your friend—Tommy, is it?— had said there would be cakes and lanterns at his place this weekend?"

"Yes, yes, Daddy! And I'm taking *my* airplane with me to Tommy's house."

Smiling, Bình found it impossible not to get caught up in his son's excitement. He remembered vividly the feeling of pure elation, heading to the Trung-Thu parade with his dream lantern. A brief glorious moment it had been, a fleeting spark of happiness whose memory had somehow survived all the sorrow and heartbreak that had followed.

"Tell you what," he said to the boy. "We'll also pick up a couple of boxes of mooncakes on the way out. They'll go on Grandpa's altar first, but after we have finished lighting candles and incense and saying a prayer for him, you may take some with you to Tommy's house."

"But can I eat some at home before I go, with you and Mommy and Grandma?"

"Now, that's an excellent idea. Then while we're having mooncakes, Mommy can tell you all the legends of Trung-Thu, and Grandma and I will share more of Grandpa's stories with you. I'm sure she will like that very much. And so will I."

"Yay! Me too, Daddy! Oh, I can't wait."

As his son looked on breathlessly, Bình reached up and unhooked the glimmering lantern from its hanger. Gazing down into the boy's eyes, filled with wonder, he caught a glimpse of the scrawny kid of long ago who had been so anxious to show his father his prized possession. It struck him in that instant just how much he had missed Ba, his protective angel in a red beret—what a huge and unfilled void his untimely departure had left in their hearts.

"It's a real beauty, this one," Bình said softly, gliding his fingertips across the glossy red paper. "And it looks just like the airplanes Grandpa and his soldier friends used to jump out of. If he were here with us today, I have no doubt he would have picked it out himself—specially for *you*, his grandson."

In the Shadow of Green Bamboos

From his patio chair a few steps away, Dean watches his wife dozing in her chaise lounge. Elise's petite frame lies barely discernible under a throw from which childlike socked feet stick out into the dappling sunlight, a paperback opened face-down on her lap with a pair of reading glasses perched crookedly atop it. A tender smile crinkles the tails of his blue eyes and deepens the grooves around his mouth. Time has been nothing but kind to her, he acknowledges once again, as he admires her delicate features framed by a cloud of soft gray hair, their exotic loveliness a reminder of the tropical land where she came from. It never ceases to amaze him how, after nearly half a century of marriage, he's still discovering something new about his wife, minute though it may be, every time he gazes at her beloved face.

As if sensing her husband's stare, Elise stirs under the throw, and her eyes flutter open. The cozy tableau of this late spring day

in a back garden outside Washington D.C. suddenly comes to life. Stretching languorously, Elise takes some deep breaths then wiggles herself up into a half-reclined position, her head tilted toward Dean. "How long have you been out here?" she mumbles with a groggy smile. "Did I doze away the whole afternoon?"

Dean pulls his chair up closer. "That's what afternoons are for, my dear," he says brightly. Then, leaning forward with a look of mixed intrigue and delight on his face, "You're aware, aren't you, that your eyes, they're shaped like bamboo leaves?"

Elise chuckles as she rubs her eyes. "My goodness. Where did that come from?"

"I never made the connection myself until this very minute." Raising a finger, Dean pushes up from his patio chair. "Be right back. A package came for you while you were resting."

Her knees drawn up, Elise watches her husband head for the screen door leading inside. His tall and robust frame, now heavier and slightly hunched over with the years, moves more slowly these days as his gait seems increasingly hampered by an old injury sustained in Việt-Nam during the war. "Stop calling it an injury, dear," he would gently correct her whenever the subject came up during conversations with relatives or acquaintances. "It was nothing more than a clumsy jump off a Huey. Only goes to show your husband was no airborne." The badly sprained ankle would have healed properly, however, had he taken the necessary time off and stayed off his feet. But being a shorthanded army doctor whose service was depended on by Special Forces camps along the Cambodian border had dictated otherwise. Still, Dean would insist the whole thing was "no biggie," dismissing it with a smiling shrug.

It's sometimes hard for Elise to believe a lifetime has passed since they first met—in Sài-Gòn, South Việt-Nam, in the sweltering summer of 1967. She had just finished high school and was struggling to support herself with a part-time gig playing the piano at a private club. The club owners, a black *métisse* who called herself Madame Yvonne and her American-contractor husband, hosted casual but elegant weekend get-togethers at their private residence with a lovely garden for invited-only guests. The patrons were mostly Americans—government workers and contractors, journalists, members of the military— all in country because of the war, which was heating up by the day. Shortly after she took Elise under her wing, Mme. Yvonne suggested to her young piano virtuoso to substitute a Western *nom de guerre* for her Vietnamese name—Thanh-Vân, or Blue Cloud—in order to facilitate interaction with her audience. As Beethoven's *Für Elise* happened to be the most popular number in her repertoire, it seemed only natural for Blue Cloud to settle on the name of the eponymous woman. "*Très bien, mon chou.* It's a great choice. Fits you perfectly," concurred an approving Mme. Yvonne.

It was in that serene setting, safely tucked in the heart of Sài-Gòn, that Elise met Dean on a Sunday in August 1967. Normally stationed at Biên-Hòa Air Base some twenty miles north of Sài-Gòn when he wasn't scuttling between Special Forces camps along the border, he happened to be on a rare visit to the capital that weekend. A journalist friend of his, Dick Hayashi, treated him to a nickel tour of the city center. They wrapped up the day with a stop at Mme. Yvonne's, where Dick was a frequent guest. Elise was there that afternoon, delighting the regulars as she always did with her repertoire run, which ended with the classic bagatelle that had spawned her new name. As she looked up from the keyboard to rousing cheers and applause—an elflike creature with a sweet, innocent smile and a pixie haircut evocative of a young Audrey Hepburn, as Dean would later recall with great fondness—her gaze locked on to his unblinking blue eyes. "I knew right then and there I was doomed," he would click his tongue and admit with a mock sigh whenever asked about how the two had met.

They began seeing each other at Mme. Yvonne's on every free weekend Dean managed to wrest from his hectic schedule. Though he denied it at first, it was transparent to his friends and Army buddies that Dean "The Lonely" Hunter—thus nicknamed when it was known he had renounced romance after receiving a "Dear John" letter from his girlfriend in the States—now seemed destined to be lonely no more.

In early 1968, as the couple's mutual affection grew, the Communists launched their Tết Offensive on South Việt-Nam, violating the Lunar New Year's ceasefire and wreaking unprece-dented death and havoc across the country. Tragedy befell countless families including Elise's, who lived in the former imperial capital of Huế, on the Central Coast. Upon getting the devastating news, she dropped everything to hurry home. In the turmoil of the Tết aftermath, the couple lost track of each other—until a year later, when Elise returned to Sài-Gòn in hopes of finding new work to support her family. The two reconnected, and this time Dean made certain they would never be separated again. He proposed. At Christmas 1970, when his extended tour ended, they traveled to Huế to get married in Elise's hometown, with all her family and close friends in attendance. After the wedding, she tearfully said goodbye to them to follow her husband to America and begin a new life with him.

Almost fifty years, one daughter and two grandchildren later, they are still happy together.

"A penny for your thoughts," says Dean, returning to his patio chair. He plops down in it and leans a flat package against the chair leg.

Elise turns to him with a rueful smile. "You remember Mme. Yvonne's garden? The bougainvillea and hibiscus arbors? It was so pretty, so peaceful. And our little group of close friends: dear, sweet Lee Anne, and Roger, and Dick and Vivienne . . . I miss them so."

"Ah, yes . . . our special getaway from all the madness." Dean lets out a long exhale. "How can I forget? The best of times, the worst of times, indeed. But what brought on the nostalgia, honey? It was the exhibition, wasn't it?"

The couple recently attended a dinner-exhibition at a local Vietnamese restaurant. It was a fundraiser for the family of a veteran of the South Vietnamese Army who had just passed away. He had also been a photographer of international fame who had won multiple awards in the 1960s and '70s. His pictures taken during military campaigns throughout South Việt-Nam had vividly captured the heartrending brutalities of war as well as the scenic beauty of the country—what was left of it. After the Communists took over in 1975, Mr. Trần was imprisoned in one of the hundreds of isolated *trại cải-tạo* ("reeducation" camps) for several years. Upon his release, he and his family escaped by boat from Việt-Nam and eventually settled in America.

At the exhibition, Elise bought reprints of a couple of his photographs that she had admired decades ago while still a young student in high school. They were both of the beautiful coastal landscape, one showing the vast, pristine sand dunes of Phan-Thiết with a tiny human silhouette crossing over the crest, and the other a bustling scene of weathered fishermen returning from the sea with their morning catch. Elise was surprised how the unadorned beauty of those forgotten pictures churned up such longing in her for a place and time that now seem to have existed only in her imagination—her childhood motherland in more peaceful times. She could hardly wait to rush home and hang the new reprints on the wall in their family room.

Dean picks up the package at his feet and hands it to her. "This little something might just cheer you up, then," he says, winking mysteriously in response to her questioning look.

Elise tears off the brown wrap paper to reveal a flat cardboard container, from which she retrieves a medium-sized picture frame. Using both hands, she lifts it out and lays it on her lap as Dean clears away the empty box and crumpled paper. Head bowed and lips slightly parted, she contemplates in silence the photograph under the Plexiglass. The bulk of the picture is bathed in a luminous shade of green, that of a tall hedge of bamboos on the side of a village road, with a bright sun illuminating it from behind. Sitting on the ground in the hedge's shadow is a young woman in a white long-sleeve shirt and baggy black pants, the typical wear of women in the Vietnamese countryside. A long shoulder pole and two baskets heaped with a colorful variety of grains and produce rest on the red dirt by her bare feet. The woman peers out from under a *nón lá*—conical straw hat—with eyes that seem to shine with contentment, perhaps for the moment of respite from the hard day's work. A classic scene from rural life in Việt-Nam.

A cutout at the bottom of the matting frames the title of the photograph in bold black print: *Dưới Bóng Tre Xanh*, or *In the Shadow of Green Bamboos*.

"You like it?" Dean asks, a hint of anxiousness in his voice. "You were staring at it for a long time at the exhibition the other night."

"It's stunning," she says quietly. "I love it."

"I was surprised when you didn't choose to buy it at the end of the evening. So I went back and got it for you." Dean shakes his head and chortles. "I asked to have it delivered to the house just so I could watch your face when it arrived. But, of course, you had to take a nap, didn't you?"

Elise reaches for his hand and squeezes it. "Thanks, honey. That's really sweet of you."

But something in her voice and demeanor catches Dean's attention. He leans in closer to the chaise lounge. "It's the same picture you admired, isn't it?"

Straightening up against the backrest, Elise breathes a soft sigh. "It's the picture all right. And it's lovely. But I didn't count on it bringing back so many memories, some of which I'd just as soon forget." Her finger slowly traces the contour of the conical straw hat in the photograph. "It happened a long time ago, and I told only one person at the time. But it's all come back so vividly in the last couple of days since I saw the picture at the exhibition." Setting the glass frame down next to her, she weaves her hands together in front of her knees and looks up at her husband with a pensive expression. "Maybe that means it's time the story gets told."

Dean drops back in his chair. His eyes, gentle and patient, remain fixed on her. Staring past him into the sunny garden beyond, Elise gathers her thoughts for a moment, then begins.

"It was spring 1968, right after the Tết Offensive. Do you remember those crazy days, how horrible and chaotic things were? There was so much death and mayhem everywhere, far worse than anything I had seen before. My hometown Huế had been engulfed in some of the fiercest fighting since the First Day of Tết. As you know, I was in Sài-Gòn at the time, only nineteen and alone in the midst of all that madness, and worried sick about my family whom I hadn't heard from in over two months. It was not until after the South Vietnamese and American forces had seized back control of Huế that the news began to filter out. Details soon followed about the horrific massacre that had taken place inside the Old Citadel. And when the full extent and atrocity of it was laid bare for all to see, it shocked the whole nation. That was when I learned that my father had been among the thousands of innocent civilians rounded up and executed by the Việt-Cộng during their brief occupation of the city. . . ."

Even though Dean has general knowledge of these circumstances, he simply nods without saying a word. Elise has never tried to keep this dark chapter in her life from him, but it's not often that she discusses it in much detail, either. It seems obvious to him that her mind, for whatever reason triggered by the captivating photograph, has been roiling with the memory of those turbulent times. If it helps her to open up about it, he's all ears.

"It was a really scary and painful time for me, and confusing as all get-out," continues Elise, now breathing faster, color rising in her cheeks. "I was at my wit's end, with no one to turn to for advice or support. Sài-Gòn itself was on lockdown, and I had no way of contacting you or Roger or Dick or getting in touch with our friends at Mme. Yvonne's. Thank goodness, though, she actually came looking for me as soon as things began to quiet down, and the citywide curfew was partially lifted. She was out making the rounds to find out how all of us girls who worked for her were doing, if we had survived the months-long knock-down, drag-out fighting.

"I've told you before, honey, and I will say it again, what a true angel she is, Mme. Yvonne. When she heard of my family situation, she went straight to her husband, Mr. Bill, and asked if he could help. Being a government contractor to MACV, he managed to pull some strings to get me a seat on the earliest flight to Phú-Bài Airport in Huế, shortly after the city had been liberated from the Communists. That was the only reason I was able to fly home to my family as early as March that year. Aside from Mme. Yvonne and Mr. Bill, who drove me to Tân-Sơn-Nhất Airport, I didn't have the chance to say goodbye to anyone else."

Dean shifts in his chair. "Ah, yes . . . I remember it like yesterday—how my heart just sank when I heard the news from Yvonne after you had already left," he says thoughtfully, now drawn back into the past himself. "I had been stuck at Special Forces camps along the Cambodian border and had no way of getting back to you. Thank goodness indeed you had Yvonne and Bill watching out for you and coming to your rescue. I was immensely relieved and grateful to them for that." On a more personal note, Dean recalls with a twinge of fresh nostalgia how despondent and hopeless he became after Elise was gone, for he had the gnawing fear that their paths might never cross again. In those times of great uncertainty, it wasn't all that uncommon for people to simply vanish into the fog of war, not to be seen or heard from ever again.

Elise's gaze follows a hummingbird from the nearby feeder to the rosebush in the corner of the small garden, yet seemingly lost in another world. "By then, it had been over three years since my last trip home," she resumes in a soft voice, so soft Dean has to strain to catch her every word. "I was very homesick. Often in my dreams, I had wandered the city's narrow streets under the red blooms of poinciana trees or crossed the Tràng-Tiền Bridge over the Perfume River. Growing up, I used to love that view of Huế from the bridge: the winding river and surrounding mountains, the temples and royal mausoleums along the banks, the Old Citadel to the north and the ocean to the east.... Every time I crossed the bridge, I would slow down just a little to take in the sight, to enjoy the cool breeze that carried over the sound of bells from Thiên-Mụ Pagoda and the fragrance of plumeria blossoms and orchard flowers from upstream. Later, when I went away to Sài-Gòn, in my naïve young mind, I had taken for granted that Huế would always be there waiting for me—always as lovely as I had remembered her. My next trip back, I had told myself again and again during those lonely years away, would be a joyful reunion with both my family and my hometown, a truly special occasion to look forward to."

She turns to Dean, her face veiled in sadness. "And then, of course, Tết happened. For all of us who lived through it, our worlds were upended and wrecked practically overnight."

At a loss for the proper words of comfort, Dean shakes his head in sympathetic silence. But he totally understands his wife's feelings of longing and regret, for he has been familiar with her unique story since their auspicious encounter in Sài-Gòn all those years ago.

Elise was born into a family of privilege in Huế, the former imperial capital of Việt-Nam. Her father was the grandson of a senior mandarin at the imperial court, and he had achieved high status in the city as a successful and well-to-do businessman. He had also done well in marriage, having wed a *Công Tôn-Nữ*, a great-granddaughter of an emperor from the waning years of the nineteenth century. The elite couple had been blessed with a first daughter—Elise—followed by two young sons. Among Elise's blue-blood cousins on her mother's side were Bảo-Đại, the last emperor of Việt-Nam from the Nguyễn Dynasty, and Madame Nhu, the formidable "Dragon Lady" who reigned over South Việt-Nam's political scene in the early sixties.

Beautiful and musically talented, Elise grew up the apple of her parents' eyes. It was never a secret that her father harbored high hopes and ambitions for his precocious daughter. And so, the year she turned fourteen, he made the difficult decision over protest from her worried mother to send her to stay with relatives in Sài-Gòn. This was to afford her the best education money could buy. To that goal, she enrolled at Lycée Marie Curie, the exclusive French high school attended by the capital's upper-class young ladies. It was expected that upon graduation, she would sit for, and pass with flying colors, the competitive entrance exam to the National Music Conservatory. There, according to her father's aspirations for her, she would receive the necessary guidance to fully develop her budding talent and groom her for a career as a concert pianist.

But as Dean's journalist friend, Dick Hayashi, quoted when he answered Dean's inquiry about Elise, "the best-laid plans of mice and men often go awry." In her final year at the Lycée, the innocent young woman with a romantic bent from Huế fell hopelessly for a handsome and charming music teacher originally from the south of France. Before long, the two got caught up in a torrid and reckless love affair that erupted into a scandal and became gossip fodder among the upper social strata in both capitals, Sài-Gòn and Huế. It all came to a crashing halt when the school, in a last-ditch attempt to safeguard its reputation, hurriedly transferred the French teacher out of the country and removed Elise from its student roster. Angered and humiliated by the dishonor she had heaped on the family, her father disowned her, despite tearful pleas from her distraught mother. To add to her troubles, the relatives who had provided Elise with room and board asked her to move out after her father cut off her financial support.

Subsisting on a meager income from a string of odd jobs, combined with what little help her mother managed to sneak to her behind her father's back, Elise landed the piano-playing gig at Mme. Yvonne's, thanks to a kind-hearted acquaintance, just in the nick of time.

From intimate conversations they shared at Mme. Yvonne's when he could swing by on the weekends, Dean learned that despite all the heartbreaks and trials, Elise still loved and missed her family and wished to someday reconcile with her father, maybe once the wounds had had time to heal. But when Tết broke out like a storm of wildfire that consumed everything in its path, not only did it wreak death and destruction over her beloved hometown Huế, it also reduced to ashes any hopes Elise had nurtured of putting things right with her father. So it doesn't surprise Dean in the least that the mere mention of Tết, even now, can still stir up such strong emotions in her.

But he can't help but wonder what unknown anecdote associated with the photograph has provoked all this spontaneous reminiscing. As if reading his mind, she takes a deep and slightly shaky inhale, lets it out slowly, then forges ahead with the narrative.

"Even with everything I had heard on the news, I was stunned on my return to find Huế such a devastated war zone. It was a flashback to those old black-and-white documentary photos of the ruined cities in Europe after World War II. The level of destruction was comparable there, in Huế. The Tràng-Tiền Bridge had collapsed into the river. The Forbidden City had been razed by heavy shelling and intense street-to-street combat, its historical monuments all crumbled or severely damaged, as were the buildings and houses in the modern sections of the city. There was this air, this dreadful, stinging smell of burn and death that hung over everything. I was absolutely heartbroken.

My old hometown that I had loved had died a violent death, buried under the rubble, along with thousands of other innocent victims. But at least we were not alone in our grief, the citizens of Huế; the entire nation was also in shock and in deep mourning for her.

"My father's remains had been recovered from a schoolyard in Gia-Hội District, just one of a number of makeshift mass graves left behind by the Communists upon their hasty retreat from the city. He had been identified by a tattered shirt that had belonged to him, his sandals and his glasses, and a small medallion of the Buddha he used to carry on him for good luck. My family had held off the funeral to wait for me. We laid him to rest as soon as I made it home. Never had I imagined my homecoming under such circumstances. It was more than I could bear, the notion that I would never get to speak with my father again, let alone ask for his forgiveness. . . ."

Elise's voice trembles as it trails off. Dean pulls his chair close to the chaise and reaches for her hands. They feel small and cold, like a child's, with a slight tremor that reminds him of a bird caught in the rain. He covers them in his hands, wishing to impart some of his own body warmth.

"We don't have to do this now, sweetheart," he says softly. "How about we go inside, and I will make us some hot jasmine tea?"

Eyes half-closed, Elise shakes her head without a word. A moment passes before she opens her eyes again and gives her husband a tiny smile. "I'm all right, thank you," she says, drawing another long breath to try to get her emotions under control. "I would rather go on if you don't mind? I'm just afraid if I stop now, I may never finish the story."

Dean nods in silence and lets go of her hands as Elise continues in a calmer voice.

"My family's house inside the Old Citadel had been badly wrecked, and it was no longer safe to stay there. Luckily, some cousins of my father who lived in Hương-Thủy District just south of Huế were kind enough to offer us their hospitality, which we accepted with gratitude.

"At the height of the Tết Battle, Cousin Lý and her elderly mother had had to evacuate for some time, but eventually they had made it through the whole ordeal safely. Even their ancestral home along National Road 1A had survived the fighting without heavy damage, a miracle in itself. And then, by chance, they learned of our dire situation. The two of them didn't think twice about opening their hearts and their home to us. If not for them, we probably would have ended up in some overcrowded relief shelter, with nowhere else to go.

"It wasn't a big house they lived in, Cousin Lý and her mother. But it must have been well built to have withstood the years and the war thus far. From its traditional architecture, it had to be close to a century old, with an austere but dignified air about it. Oh, sweetheart, I can't even tell you how blessed and comforting it felt to know that once again we had a sound roof over our heads, four solid walls around us with no rocket holes to let the cold wind through, and a front door that we could close and latch any time we needed to. It would take a long while for life to return to normal for all of us, but in the meantime, we thanked our lucky stars, and our dear cousins, for what we had.

"Our temporary residence was located in a semi-rural area southwest of Phú-Bài Airport. In its heyday in the past century, it must have been a sight to see, surrounded by old villages, rice paddies, and gardens of betel nut palm trees. But over time, the city had encroached on the area and transformed most of the pastoral landscape. A few vestiges of it still remained, though, among them a tall hedge of bamboos directly across the National Road from the house."

Elise pauses to pick up the framed photograph, holding it with both hands at chest height. She contemplates the picture for a moment, lost in memories. Dean discreetly sits back in his chair and stretches his legs, waiting. His movement seems enough to break the spell as Elise lays down the frame, leans back against her chaise, and nodding at Dean, resumes her story.

"The hedge of bamboos in Hương-Thủy—whose name means 'perfumed waters'—looked a lot like the one photographed here. That was what struck me immediately when I first stumbled across the picture at the exhibition. And what lovely hedges they both were: twenty to thirty feet tall at least, wide and thick, and so vibrant-looking with their shiny green leaves and stalks. I just love the contrast between the shadow and the hot, bright sun behind the trees, so perfectly captured in the photo.

You can almost feel the breeze rubbing the smooth stalks against each other and hear the birds chirping in the foliage. There's nothing more evocative of a peaceful afternoon in the Vietnamese countryside than this idyllic scene. All that's missing to make the scene come alive is the sound of a rooster crowing or a boy playing the flute while tending his water buffalo.

"Anyway, it seemed a true miracle to all of us that the bamboo hedge in Hương-Thủy, like our cousins' house, had escaped the brutal months-long fighting pretty much unscathed. There certainly was ample evidence of fierce battle all around there: houses with roofs blown and walls pockmarked by bullet holes, charred skeletons of abandoned bicycles and scooters or of a truck turned on its side, scorched trunks and debris from roadside trees uprooted by bombs or rockets. Which explained why, whenever I could steal a quiet moment for myself, I would linger by the large window with shutters in the front room and gaze out at the bamboo hedge across the road, imagining a more innocent and happier time in the past.

"The front room was small and dark, even with the window, and dominated by a massive teak cabinet with mother-of-pearl inlays. The place of honor atop the cabinet had been set up for use as the ancestral altar. The cousins were gracious enough to invite us to place a picture of my late father up there, among several faded black-and-white photos of long-deceased ancestors, a pair of red candles in sculpted brass holders, and a ceramic bowl of incense. There were empty plates on the altar that would normally hold offerings of fresh fruit, along with an antique vase devoid of the traditional marigold flowers—all signs of the hard times we had experienced since Tết. The pungent aroma from a century of incense burning pervaded the room, like inside the hallways of a Buddhist temple. Every time I stepped into the room, I would find myself instantly transported to a bygone place and time. But that was where I slept at night, sharing a double-sized cot below the window with Cousin Lý since we barely had enough room in the small house to accommodate the six of us."

Deeply immersed in recollections, Elise takes a momentary pause.

"Can I get you something to drink, honey?" Dean asks, half rising. "Iced tea? Water?"

Eyes burning bright as if to pierce further through the veil of memory, she shakes her head to signal she would rather keep going. Dean drops back down.

"Cousin Lý was five or six years older than me, and I loved her like the big sister I never had. She was kind, quiet, and thoughtful, and a great sounding board for me on just about any subject. Which was what I desperately needed then, with my mother too distraught to handle the day-to-day concerns, and my two brothers still too young. And so the bulk of decisions for our makeshift household fell on Cousin Lý and me, and that brought us even closer.

"In those months following Tết, power outages were the rule. We would try to finish dinner by six o'clock and turn in a couple of hours later, before it got real dark, to save on candles and kerosene. After hanging the mosquito net over our cot, Cousin

Lý and I would lie down and talk over the day for a few minutes before going to sleep.

"On this particular night, I was feeling unusually restless and had trouble falling asleep. To make matters worse, it was hot and stuffy, especially with the door and all the windows closed. Tossing and turning next to Cousin Lý, I could hear her regular breathing in her deep sleep, the scratching noise of rodents chasing each other on the rafters, the sound of crickets right outside the window—even the *thump-thump* of my own heartbeat. My thoughts were racing nonstop from one thing to the next, and I felt crushed by the burden of grief and worry." Elise turns to Dean, a wistful look in her eyes. "I was still mourning the death of my father, but I was also missing you dearly because I thought I would never see you again. At the same time, the future appeared so uncertain and hopeless, for me as well as my family. All of a sudden my eyes welled up with tears and I had to hurry and roll over on my side, facing away from Cousin Lý. . . ."

Elise's voice wavers a little but steadies itself as Dean reaches over to take her hands again. Holding on to his gentle grip, she clears her throat then continues.

"The tears just kept on coming. Even gritting my teeth, I could not stop them, and soon I was sobbing quietly. Afraid that I might wake Cousin Lý, I crawled up and snuck out from under the mosquito net. Then, as gingerly as possible, I unlatched the shutters on the window above the cot and pushed them open. Cooler air swept into the room. I immediately felt better.

"It was dark outside, but not pitch-black. There was a quarter moon half-hidden behind high clouds, and I could see out to the National Road, some fifty yards from the house. The road was covered in dust, and it looked slick and silvery like a snake under the pale moonlight. Beyond it, on the far side, loomed the tall and thick bamboo hedge of Hương-Thủy Village.

"And then I heard it. Barely above the crickets at first, then rising higher and more distinct by the moment. The sound of a woman crying. More like wailing, actually. Just loud enough to carry through the night and make the hair on the back of my neck stand up. And even though I couldn't make out any words, the sorrow in her voice was so stark and unmistakable it tore at my heart and ripped it to pieces.

"I stood and peered out into the night, searching. It was much darker now, for the moon had slipped completely behind the clouds. The front yard—the wide, empty space between the house and the road, overgrown with dead weeds—looked deserted. Suddenly my eyes, squinting and straining, picked up movement across the road, by the black shadow that was the bamboo hedge. Was it some animal? A person? I could not tell. But my heart was pounding right out of my chest. What if it was the Việt-Cộng creeping back into town under the cover of darkness?

"But before I could react, a loud crackling noise startled me. Then the whole area in front of the house lit up in a flickering yellow light. I blinked, frozen in place. It turned out to be a couple of flares exploding in the sky, as happened regularly throughout each night.

"I breathed in relief and blinked again—then I saw her. The woman by the bamboo hedge.

"She was dressed in the traditional black pants and long-sleeve shirt of working women in the countryside and carried a long pole over her shoulder with a basket swinging from each end. Exactly like the woman in the picture, but without the conical straw hat. It must have fallen off somewhere along the way, in her rush. For she was dashing about in obvious panic, her hair and clothes completely disheveled. It was she crying out there, wailing in distress. What was she running from at this late hour? And where to? Why all the agony? All kinds of questions popped into my head. Meanwhile, she kept circling the bamboo hedge while scrutinizing the ground as if looking for something. Something of great value that she had lost? Whatever the circumstances, it was clear the poor woman could use some help.

"I was about to go light a kerosene lamp and head out toward her, when she stopped dead in her tracks and looked up in my direction. She must have seen me watching her from the window. Dropping the shoulder pole and its load baskets to the ground, she darted across the road toward the house, her hands up in the air and waving frantically. It appeared she was shouting out to me, but all I could hear was her gut-wrenching sobs. Oh, those cries . . . they rattled my nerves and brought tears to my eyes all over again. As she got to the middle of the front yard, I was staring straight at her, and I could see, as clearly as I'm seeing you now, honey"—Elise shudders at the recollection—"her eyes, so haggard and desperate—and her stained face, twisted in pain. . . .

"Then suddenly everything went black. I jumped and barely suppressed a yelp. It was as if I had been struck blind momentarily. And then it dawned on me: it was only the flares burning out. The next moment, a swirl of cold—I mean, *really* frigid—air blew in through the window past me, or right through me, to be precise. It made me gasp and sent shivers up and down my back, giving me goosebumps all over. I remember thinking how odd this was since it had been unusually warm and muggy all evening. By the time the mass of cold air had passed into the night—it couldn't have been more than seconds, although it seemed much longer— my head was swimming, and my ears were buzzing with an electric, tinny sound. I was drenched in sweat and feeling drained and had to lean against the window to catch my breath.

"I was still pulling myself together when I noticed the front yard brightening again. Gradually, but pretty fast all the same. The moon had reemerged from behind the clouds to light up the landscape once more. I craned my neck out the window and scanned the entire space in front of the house but found no trace of the mysterious woman anywhere. Not in the front yard, nor near the bamboo hedge. The shoulder pole and the baskets had disappeared, too. I searched up and down the road as far as my eyes could see. No sign of any traffic, foot or otherwise. The woman had simply vanished like the wind. It was dead quiet and utterly still all around, except for the usual sounds of the night.

"I checked several more times again before giving up eventually. It was getting quite late, and I was too shaken up and exhausted to try and make sense of what I had just witnessed. So I hastily closed the shutters, made sure the latch was secured, and hustled back inside the mosquito net. Cousin Lý had hardly stirred from her earlier position, which thankfully meant that she had not been disturbed by all the goings-on. At least one of us was getting some much-needed rest. Still shaking inside, I quickly fell into a deep, heavy sleep, which was filled with all sorts of strange and scary dreams. I woke up the next morning aching all over, with a monstrous headache to boot. . . ."

Elise's shoulders sag; she brings her hands up and rubs her eyes, breathing rapidly.

"May I have that iced tea now, please?" she finally says, her voice a raspy whisper.

"Coming right up," says Dean, who has gotten up and gone over to stand next to his wife's chaise. He ambles into the house and reappears a short while later, carrying a folding tray table with two glasses on it. Setting it down by Elise's chaise, he hands her one of the cold drinks with a napkin and takes the other one back to his seat with him. She drinks several long drafts from the sweating, tall glass, relishing each one of them, then replaces it on the tray, a tad more than half empty. Using the napkin, she takes a moment to dab her lips dry.

"Thank you, hon," she says with a smile, apparently satiated and refreshed. Dean winks at her, raises his glass, and downs another gulp of iced tea. Sitting back up with her arms wrapped around her bent knees, Elise continues with her story, her voice stronger and steadier now.

"When I got up the next day feeling out of sorts, my percep-tive cousin took notice of it right away. She approached me and asked if I was doing all right.

"'Ô, I'm fine, thank you,' I lied. 'Did you sleep well last night, Chị Lý?'

"'I was out, dead to the world,' she said, chuckling. 'The only thing that could have woken me up would be a rocket exploding in the front yard, which we pray shall never happen.'

"The events of the previous night were still vivid in my mind, but in the broad daylight, they now felt unreal, even ludicrous— like something out of a fantastical dream or the product of an overactive imagination. All the more since there was no other witness than me. So I thought it best to set the whole thing aside and not breathe a word of it to anyone, Cousin Lý included. Together, we went about our day as usual, and I soon forgot all about the incident.

"That is, until the evening came.

"In the looming darkness and fluttering candlelight, the memory of the night before rushed back in eerie detail, and try as I might, I was unable to get those sounds and images out of my head. As I was helping Cousin Lý hang the mosquito net over the cot in preparation for bedtime, I was seized anew with apprehension. Then later, after we had gone to lie down, I tried to keep the unsettled feeling at bay by chatting my cousin's ear off until she couldn't help it anymore and dozed off. As I lay wide awake next to her, my anxiety mounted. The hours ticked by. My body tensed up at every little noise, and at times I caught myself holding my breath just so I could listen more attentively. But my ears detected nothing out of the ordinary, only critters of the night or an occasional gust of wind. Bone-weary in the end, I succumbed to sleep in the small hours—only to be startled awake by a diligent rooster at daybreak.

"Despite the short and fitful night's rest, I felt such relief that early morning when I squinted my eyes open and saw gray daylight leaking through the shutters' slats. I had made it through the whole night without incident. It appeared that the nightmares that had so disrupted my sleep the other evening were now over. And things had returned to normal—more or less.

"I hadn't lost my marbles after all! Though Cousin Lý would probably have disagreed, I supposed, had I rushed to share my experience with her a day earlier. As it had turned out, a crisis had been averted and I had saved myself a huge embarrassment.

"The rest of the day flew by on that high note, even though I was dragging from serious lack of sleep. When we went to bed that evening, I was in good spirits and feeling relaxed, but so dead tired I must have dropped off almost immediately, which seldom happened with me.

"I had been out cold for some time, exactly how long I had no idea, when the noise crept in and roused me from a deep sleep. Even with my eyes still shut and my brain in a dense fog, I instantly recognized the woman's voice. Her cries traveled through the walls and the closed window—just as distraught and mournful as the first night, and distinct enough above the frogs and crickets to yank me out of my dreams.

"I sprang up like a shot and hit my head on the roof of the mosquito net.

"My eyes gritty from interrupted sleep, I felt my way out of the tangled net and staggered to the window. Cousin Lý, meanwhile, remained blessedly oblivious to the disturbance.

"I can't tell you what possessed me in that moment to think I should open the shutters even with my pulse racing so fast it made me lightheaded. But all I could hear, all I was tuned in to, was the voice calling to me, beckoning me forward. Pleading with me—for help, maybe?

"With shaky hands, I unlatched the shutters and nudged one of the panels open, creaking on its rusty hinges. I cringed and flattened myself behind the other panel to venture a peek outside.

"And there she was, in plain view under the soft moonlight. The mysterious crying woman. Back across the road by the bamboo hedge, wearing the same disheveled clothes as before, as if she had never gone away. Like the first time, I could make her out clearly enough, even from the distance and partially covered in shadow. My breathing stopped.

"Her shoulder pole and baskets lay tossed on the dirt while she paced frantically around the hedge, first in one direction then the other, scouring the ground and occasionally rooting among the bamboo stalks, still in search of something. Then, in obvious frustration and despair, she dropped down on the dirt on her behind and hung her head between her bent knees, her shoulders heaving in sobs. I had no idea what the situation was—where she had come from, or what great loss she had sustained that had caused her such anguish—but her wails, so grief-stricken, had me all torn up inside once again. I wanted desperately to reach out to her.

"As if reading my mind, the unknown woman slowly lifted her face and turned toward me.

"I gasped and stumbled back in the dark with a hand pressed over my mouth. My heart was pounding so wildly it shot pain through my chest, yet my unblinking eyes remained glued to her.

"In the hazy moonlight, I glimpsed what I thought was a gunshot wound to the side of her head, where the hair looked to be matted in dried blood. There were also dark stains splattered down the front of her white shirt. How could I possibly have missed any of this before? Or had she waited on purpose until this very moment to finally reveal herself to me in full?

"My blood turned cold. I froze in horror, unable to utter a single sound while at the same time powerless to turn away.

"The woman raised both arms to me, as in earnest supplication for help, and began to rise unsteadily to her feet. Out of nowhere, a breeze had picked up and was ruffling her long hair and baggy clothes and causing dead leaves to whirl around her.

"I don't know what broke the spell in that instant—perhaps just being frightened out of my wits—but somehow I mustered enough strength to reach up and pull the shutters closed, fumble with the latch to secure it in place, and scramble like crazy to crawl back inside the mosquito net. My body was shaking like a leaf. I was burning up and shivering all at once. In my blind terror, my thoughts instinctively turned to my ancestors on the altar in the center of the room, and I started praying fervently to them for protection. It had been another warm and muggy night; still, I pulled a thin cover over my head and curled up on my side with my back to the window, face burrowed in the pillow and eyes clamped shut.

"It was in that coiled position that I remained for the rest of the night, straining to listen for any approaching footsteps and jumping every time the wind rattled the shutters. I didn't sleep a wink, too anxious waiting for morning to come. . . ."

Elise pauses, her breathing short and ragged, her face taut in concentration.

Dean picks up her glass and hands it to her. "Have another sip, honey," he says soothingly. "You must be thirsty. Take your time and finish it up; I'll go get you a refill."

She accepts the glass and drinks greedily from it while her husband watches her.

"Wow," he says with a soft whistle, "what extraordinary memories you are unearthing. And such vivid recollection, too. I was right there with you."

Elise returns the empty glass to the tray, her hand covering the rim to indicate she doesn't need a refill. "How can one ever forget something like that?" she says, shaking her head. "But it has been coming back to me in greater detail over the last couple of days. I have been thinking of little else since the exhibition. At the same time, though, you can understand why I have always been leery of sharing the story with anybody.

"But after that sleepless night, I could no longer keep my secret from Cousin Lý. I just had to tell someone, or I would go out of my mind. But it had got to be someone sensible who would listen to all I had to say and not dismiss it outright. And who better than my considerate cousin? Besides, she already saw what a state I was in, and she, of all people, would know just how to draw it out of me sooner or later. But I wanted to talk to her alone, out of earshot of everybody else in the house, especially of my mother and my younger brothers. That way, we wouldn't risk frightening or upsetting them unnecessarily. The perfect opportunity presented itself when Cousin Lý asked me to walk with her to the village market later that morning.

"It was a makeshift open market assembled every other day on a vacant field gouged and charred by stray rockets, about three kilometers or a forty-five-minute hike from the house. The old market hall had been all but destroyed during the battle, not to be rebuilt for some indefinite time. The two of us set out along the National Road, donning our *nón lá*—conical straw hats— and dodging into the shade of the trees whenever possible to shield ourselves from the scorching sun.

"As understanding and thoughtful as I knew Cousin Lý to be, I still felt extremely nervous recounting my recent experiences to her, for they sounded so surreal even to my own ears. But luckily, and to my relief, she appeared to have no trouble following the story despite all my hemming and hawing, as she kept pace alongside me, nodding in silence. Only when I had finished talking did she signal for us to stop. Then, turning away from the busy road, she led us into the shade of a big tamarind tree.

" 'So,' she said, 'you had a good look at her then.' Her voice, hoarse and urgent, startled me.

" 'Yes,' I replied, somewhat defensively, 'I saw her as plainly as I would any person out there under the moonlight. But why? Have you—have *you* seen the woman, too?'

" 'No, no. I never saw her myself, but some people around here have. And they all described her exactly as you did. *Trời ơi*— good heavens. It is really true then.' She sounded shocked.

"I placed my hand on her forearm, growing more alarmed by the minute. 'What is this about, *Chị* Lý? Please tell me. You are making me nervous.'

"She leaned against the tree, took off her *nón lá* and fanned herself with it, and invited me to do the same. Then, glancing back up the road toward the tall bamboo hedge in the distance, she began to relate *her* story—all the local whispers swirling around the mysterious woman.

"According to my cousin, no one in Hương-Thủy knew who the woman was or where she had come from. Just another nameless face amid the thousands of refugees displaced by the war and fleeing south along National Road 1A during the Tết Battle. It was said she had a baby boy with her, a toddler whom she had tucked among personal belongings in one of the baskets that she carried on her shoulder pole. But as the long column of refugees draggled past the village, the woman suddenly realized that her precious load had gone missing without her knowing. In the general chaos, her baby had fallen out of the basket somewhere along the way.

"Can you imagine what a horrible shock that must have been to the mother? The poor woman just passed out cold. When she came to, she immediately proceeded to turn back to begin the search for her lost child, ignoring advice from other people to at least wait until the fighting had abated. She walked all night with the baskets on her shoulder pole and retraced her steps as far back as the tall bamboo hedge. But there, her search ended in disaster. She was caught in the crossfire of a bloody skirmish with nowhere to hide and was hit—another anonymous statistic of the Tết Offensive. Sadly, too, no one knew what had happened to the baby.

"Cousin Lý was crying now, and so was I right along with her.

"'And that would have been the tragic end to the story,' my cousin said in between sniffles, 'had it not been for the rumors that surfaced soon after the fighting was over, and people started coming home. Some villagers claimed they had sighted a woman matching the description you gave, wandering at night near the bamboo hedge. The mysterious figure is widely believed to be the mother who had lost her baby—or her restless spirit, rather. People say she still walks this stretch of the National Road looking for her child, especially on moonlit nights. And since our house sits right across the road from where she was killed, those same village folks have stopped by to share their stories with us. But neither my mother nor I have ever witnessed anything like that. To tell you the truth, we did not believe a whole lot of what we were told. At least I didn't. Not until now.'

"I was stunned speechless. On the one hand, it was a huge load off my mind to receive some validation of my experiences—to know I had not imagined things. With the entire world tossed upside down since Tết, I couldn't be too sure anymore. But on the other hand, the tragedy of this unfortunate woman and her lost baby shook me to the core. It was yet another poignant reminder of how wide and deep, how indiscriminate and close to home the suffering ran.

"And still more questions remained.

" 'But why *me*?' I mumbled, wiping my eyes. 'Why did she choose to show herself to me, not just once but twice? Was she trying to give me a message?'

"Cousin Lý thought about it, then said, 'I certainly don't claim to know any more about this sort of thing than you do. But maybe the answer is related to your personal situation: the fact that you, too, have gone through a lot of turmoil in your life recently; that you have just lost someone you loved, your father, and you are still mourning for him. Maybe that was something the woman could sense in you, something she could connect with?'

"Then she thoughtfully wagged a finger at me. 'You know what we should do, cousin?' she said. 'Let's get some fresh fruit and flowers at the market; it doesn't have to be much. Then let's take the offerings to the bamboo hedge, and you and I will light incense and say a prayer for the poor soul. That is the least we can do for her, don't you think?'

"I agreed wholeheartedly. And so, later that afternoon, after the market and then lunch, my cousin and I waited until everyone else in the house had lain down for their midday nap before we carried our meager offerings to the bamboo hedge across the road. We walked around to the backside of the hedge, out of sight of passing traffic, and set down on the dirt a small vase of marigolds and a plate of green bananas and mandarin oranges. Then, in the shadow of the tall bamboo trees, we each lit a stick of incense and said our prayers for the hapless victim.

"I closed my eyes and tried to visualize the woman again—in her disheveled clothes, with the gunshot wound to her head and the look of agony and despair on her face. With her cries still echoing in my ears, I now understood why she had sounded so heartbroken, beyond solace. Tears streamed down my face as I grieved for both of our losses, hers and mine. I prayed with all my heart that she would finally be able to move on and find peace, knowing that she had done all she could have and made the ultimate sacrifice for her child. In the afternoon breeze, I started to feel the heaviness lift off my shoulders, and with it, any residual fear from the early encounters. What remained, instead, was a peaceful feeling of kinship with the unfortunate stranger.

"Later, at bedtime that evening, Cousin Lý fought hard to stay awake and keep me company. Lying side by side on the cot with our arms draped over our foreheads, we chatted in low voices about everything under the sun—except the woman. Deep down, however, I knew we were both waiting—listening—intensely for our nocturnal visitor. But we heard nothing above the normal soothing sounds of the night, punctuated by the crackling of flares that lit up the black sky. Our talk slowly died down, and soon I could hear the rhythmic breathing of my cousin next to me. It wasn't long before I drifted off to sleep myself, my first sound sleep in a while.

"The woman never came, not that night or the next, or the night after that. I kept watching for her over the following weeks, all the while hoping and praying that she would not show—that she had moved on. It seemed my prayer was answered. I never saw or heard her again.

"We stayed with Cousin Lý and her mother until the end of that summer. It gave me time to fill out the required paperwork with my father's bank to secure enough funds for the repair of our family home in the city, at least to the point where we could move back in.

"The last time I saw my cousin, honey, was at our wedding in Huế, at Christmas 1970. You probably don't remember it with all the people there, but she came with her mother. We hugged and cried because I was leaving right afterward to come to America

with you. We have since kept in touch by correspondence—
though rather infrequently, I must admit—but not once in all
these years have we brought up the woman again. Her death, like
those of other obscure, defenseless victims of the war, was a
tragedy so heartrending, so vile and unjust, it still gnaws at us to
this day. You know, not exactly the kind of memories we're eager
to reminisce about. Yet there is one thing I'm certain of: neither
of us has ever forgotten about the woman or her baby."

Elise lets out a long breath and sags against the backrest, her legs
fully stretched out under the throw. The lines of concentration
around her eyes and her mouth begin to ease. She appears
drained, though more relaxed, having at last gotten the long-
carried burden off her chest.

Dean pulls his seat up next to her chaise and wraps his arm
around her back. She leans up against him, resting her tired eyes
and breathing softly.

"And here I thought I knew everything about you," he says
teasingly. "This is the first I've heard of those days when you were
alone in Huế after Tết, you know that? So thank you for sharing,
sweetheart." He rocks her gently in his arm. "Boy, the things
you all went through, you and your family. And your amazing
experience with the unknown woman. I myself have never heard
of anything like that, let alone witnessed it with my own eyes. It
just boggles the mind."

Her head nestled against his shoulder, Elise whispers, "Do
you often think about the ghosts of war? Mine have stuck with

me through the years, and I carry them in my heart wherever I go: my father, many of our friends at Mme. Yvonne's, and other people I knew whose lives were cut short. But this woman in Hương-Thủy was different. She was a total stranger to me, yet her story touched something deep in me. I have always remembered her. And even though I hadn't thought much about her in years, all it took to bring her back was a chance glance at this picture at the exhibition. And then I got hit with this nagging feeling all over again, like there must have been something, however little, that I could have done for her and her baby back then. Isn't that crazy, seeing that I wasn't even around there when she got killed?"

Dean positions himself so he can look his wife in the eyes. "What you and your cousin did for the woman was truly a thoughtful and compassionate gesture. It wasn't so much the incense or the offerings as the fact that someone cared enough to acknowledge what she had endured—her great loss and her agony. That, in a way, should have given her some measure of justice and comfort. I'd really love to believe that. Things being what they were, there wasn't anything else you could have done for her except to honor her memory and her suffering, the way you all did."

He pauses to gaze out at the garden in the late afternoon sunlight before continuing, "And yes, me too, I've carried my many ghosts around with me. Not so that I can dwell on regrets of what could have been or torment myself with survivor's guilt, mind you. This may sound a bit hokey, but I made up my mind long ago to honor their memory by not letting myself forget how precious life is, and by trying to appreciate it to the fullest." Then, winking at his wife, whose tender eyes are fixed on him, " 'Trying' is the operative word here, for we both well know it's not always as easy as it sounds. Don't we, dear? But one thing for sure: having you by my side through all the ups and downs over the years has been a tremendous godsend and a lifesaver, more than I can ever say."

Clearing his throat, Dean picks up the framed photograph and stares at it for a long minute. Then, with a warm smile, he passes it to his wife. "I've never been much of a photog myself, and not for lack of interest either. But even to my layman's eyes, this is world-class stuff. The picture captures everything just perfectly: the play of light and shadow over the vibrant colors, the contented expression on the woman's face, the rustic serenity. It transports me right back to your beautiful ancestral homeland— without the fighting, of course. I just hope you can fully enjoy it for what it is, honey, and not allow nightmarish memories of long ago to detract from its beauty or its sentimental value to you. It would be a real shame if they did."

Elise gazes at the photograph. Her eyes trace and linger over every detail, taking it all in as if for the first time. After a while, she looks up at her husband and slowly nods, returning his smile. "You are right. This brings back wonderful memories of childhood summers spent at my grandparents' house in the countryside. And that's what I want to hold on to for as long as I can. We also bought two other pictures from the exhibition with gorgeous scenery just like this one. Perhaps we can hang them all together as a set in the main hallway, right there among the collage of photos of Clara, Billy, and the grandkids? It would be a nice way to pay tribute to the photographer, Mr. Trân. Don't you think?"

"But of course. Excellent idea, sweetie," says Dean, beaming with excitement. "Just show me exactly where you want them hung, and it shall be done. And right in time for next month's big reunion with our friends from the war days. Yvonne and Bill have already confirmed they'll be driving up from Atlanta. Roger, his boy Sơn, and Sơn's family will fly in from California, as will Paul 'The Kid' from Iowa. Even Bob Olsen's widow, Nancy, from Minnesota, has said she would love to come and meet everyone. If I'm not mistaken, it's also likely that her son Eric and his family will accompany her. Can you imagine? The first time we're all getting together. With the younger generations, too. It'll be quite a group, a truly memorable occasion. Truthfully, I never thought I'd see the day." Slapping his thighs, he bounces out of his chair. "Hey, the sun is dropping fast. It's getting a bit nippy out here. How about some hot jasmine tea now?"

Stretching languorously, Elise reaches her hands up to Dean, and he helps her up off the chaise. Then, his arm wrapped around her back and his free hand grasping the framed picture, they amble side by side toward the sliding glass door.

"I've told you, haven't I, kiddo," he pulls her in closer and whispers in her ear, "your pretty eyes, they're shaped like bamboo leaves."

Of Crickets and Dragons*

"What am I going to tell Má if I get hungry later?" asked Cu Bi (Coo-Bee), six, whose nickname means "little marbles" in Vietnamese, as he yanked nervously on his brother's hand. His perky, round eyes, which had earned him the nickname, shone with anxiety under a tan forehead and a crop of uneven black hair that stuck up like weeds in places.

Cu Tí (Coo-Tee), or "baby mouse," older by two years though barely a couple of inches taller on legs as scrawny as his little brother's, squeezed his hand back. "Hey. You're *not* going to be hungry. I will share my *xôi*—sweet rice—with you as we talked about. Promise."

The sun was already high on that summer morning of 1968 as the two boys held hands and tiptoed around the mud puddles that dotted the open food market behind their neighborhood.

* An earlier edition of this story was published in the *Louisville Review* 40th Anniversary Issue, Volume 80, Fall 2016.

The backs of their shorts and bare legs were splattered with mud stains kicked up from their rubber sandals in their hurry to get there. It had poured rain overnight, but the clouds had long since vaporized, unveiling a hazy blue sky. The muggy air was baking, as could be expected in Sài-Gòn in August, at the peak of the monsoon season. But that didn't seem to deter in the least the noisy rabble that assembled every morning at the makeshift market on the vacant lot.

Pulling his little brother by the hand, Cu Tí threaded his way among the hodgepodge of steamy food carts and baskets strewn all over the ground. Once a week, their mother gave each of them five *đồng* to treat themselves to their favorite breakfast at the market—sweet rice with yellow mung bean, sprinkled with shredded coconut and brown sugar and served on a banana leaf. But on that morning, sweet rice with mung bean and coconut, as delicious as it always sounded, wasn't the first thing on the boys' minds. In fact, whispering under their shared blanket the night before so they wouldn't be heard by their parents, they had made a secret pact: they would order just a single portion of sweet rice in the morning and split it between the two of them. The money they saved, the boys were dying to spend on something else.

"There he is," shouted Cu Tí, flailing his skinny arm at an old-looking man squatting on his haunches in a far corner. The man was clothed in a peasant's black pajamas with a red-and-white kerchief tied around his head, and on the ground next to him sat what looked like a small cage. The brothers took off trotting toward the man and dropped to their hands and knees in front of the cage. It was a rough-hewn wooden box, taller and wider than it was deep, with a fine mesh screen tightly stretched across its front. The screen was crawling with critters on the inside, and a concert of high chirping sounds emanated from the box.

"Look here," exclaimed Cu Tí, poking excitedly at the metallic web with his finger.

The younger boy twisted his body, hunkering down lower with his head between his knees as he strained to follow. "Where? Where? Which one?"

"Right here, see it? This giant red one. A real mean-looking fire cricket!"

Cu Bi traced his finger over the screen, his mouth agape in wonder at the squirming variety and multitude. "How about that black one?" he yelled, pointing. "*Bự dễ sợ*—it's *huge*."

His big brother nodded with knowledgeable appreciation. "A-ha, that's a coal cricket. Not too bad. Fire crickets are a lot tougher, though."

"We getting the other one then?" the younger boy asked.

Cu Tí looked up at the old man. "How much?" he said, holding his breath.

"Six *đồng*," said the man nonchalantly, as he gauged their reaction.

The brothers' shoulders drooped. "But we only have five," mumbled Cu Bi.

The old man held out his hand, black and wizened from the years and weather. As his little brother watched anxiously, Cu Tí handed over a fistful of pre-counted coins and crumpled bills.

"Which one?" the man said, shoving the money into his pajama pocket. His other hand slid open a small hatch at the top of the cage and plunged into the chirping swarm inside.

"This one, this one," the boys shouted in unison, springing up on their knees and frantically jabbing at the screen in chase of their flitting target. As if guided by an invisible eye on the back of his hand, the old man deftly cupped his fingers around the prized critter and lifted it from the cage, closing the hatch with a flick of his elbow.

He opened his fist just enough for the eager brothers to get a peek and verify that it was the one. "Good pick, boys," he said, nodding approvingly. "Best of the bunch. He's a sure winner."

Rooting through a bag at his feet, the man retrieved an empty matchbox and cracked it open to drop the cricket inside before pushing the box shut again. He delivered the precious load into Cu Tí's waiting hand. "Remember. Only feed him fresh grass, you hear?" he instructed the boys, who listened attentively with wide eyes. "Make a bed of sand, then leave the matchbox cover on it so he has a little nook to crawl in. Them crickets like it dark. The darker, the better."

For the rest of the morning, the boys busied themselves building a home for their new pet out of a discarded shoebox and a little sand begged from Ông Ba, the neighborhood's handyman. After sprinkling the sand bed with blades of fresh grass harvested from the roadsides of their neighborhood, they released the fire cricket into its new den. Cu Bi observed in silence his brother roll a ball of backyard mud onto the end of a long toothpick.

"What you making?" he whispered, curiosity finally getting the better of him.

Cu Tí held up the toothpick at eye level, slowly rolled it around between his fingers for careful inspection, then blew on the mud to dry it, his eyes squinting in concentration.

"Watch," he mouthed as he gingerly removed the shoebox lid.

The boys' heads leaned in together over the open box on the floor.

In a corner on the sand bed, next to the hollow matchbox cover, crouched the red-winged critter, immobile right down to the tips of its long antennae.

Cu Bi's eyes grew as big as two longan seeds. "He *dead*?" he said breathlessly.

Lips set tight, his brother slowly advanced the mud ball toward the frozen cricket.

In a flash, the critter's wings flared out around its arched body, furiously rubbing against each other to sound a shrill warning. Its antennae now flipped forward, the cricket bared its mandibles like a pair of threatening fangs, ready to pounce on the intruding mud ball.

The boys jumped back in tandem, shrieking.

"You see *that*?" yelled Cu Tí, hopping up and down triumphantly while brandishing his toothpick lance. "What did I say, ha? He's going to win all his fights. A real champ, this one."

The younger boy's eyebrows knitted. "What fights?" he asked.

"I'm going to take him to fight all the other kids' crickets," announced his brother. "And he's going to beat every single one of them. Just you wait and see."

Cu Bi crawled back over the shoebox for another close-up peek.

"What if the other ones bite off his legs or his whiskers? Or he gets killed?" he said.

Ever since Tết in late January when the Vietnamese New Year's celebration had exploded into fierce combat, Cu Bi's head had been flooded with frightening images of death and havoc. The television news had shown them one after another, and the worried adults couldn't seem to talk about anything else. And then just last month one of the neighbor kids had lost his father, a South Vietnamese army officer killed in battle by the Việt-Cộng.

Cu Bi did not want his cricket to get killed or broken, in any way. Not at all.

"Let's don't fight him," he pleaded with his big brother. "Can we just keep him and feed him fresh grass every day? That's plenty fun for me." Then, in a last-ditch effort to distract the older boy from his plan, "What are we going to name him?"

"*Name*?" Cu Tí said. "Nobody names a cricket. And don't be a baby now." He carefully replaced the lid over the box. He had

known, from having observed other kids, to punch holes in the
lid to let air through. "He's unbeatable, I tell you. A real champ."
Then he grabbed Cu Bi by the hand and pulled him up. "Let's go
eat. I'm starved."

In the afternoon, the younger boy tried several more times to
change his brother's mind, to no avail. So when bedtime rolled
around, Cu Bi was squirming with nerves.

The boys slept on a straw mat on the floor underneath their
bed, which had been raised on sandbags to serve as a poor man's
bunker against nightly rocket attacks by the Việt-Cộng. Cu Bi
always chose to slide in first next to the wall. It made him feel
safer to be wedged between the solid wall on one side and his big
brother on the other. In addition, the two shared a thin blanket
that he could pull over his head for extra protection. Thus, safely
cocooned, he usually fell asleep before his brother did, which was
what he hoped for. But on this stifling summer night, he was still
wiggling around long after Cu Tí lay still.

In the dark, the young boy felt deep rumblings through the
ground from bomb chains being dropped all around the outskirts
of Sài-Gòn. It was the same every evening, and the brothers had
taken to telling each other, as a fun bedtime story to fall asleep
to, that it was a herd of elephants tromping out of the jungle, on
their way down to the river for a late-night drink. Once in a
while, a frantic curfew-patrol siren pierced the night before
trailing off into the distance, in urgent pursuit of some ghostly,

dangerous intruders. The air was crackling with tension, but all Cu Bi could think of, all he could see, even with his eyes squeezed shut, was the dismembered body of his cricket after a brutal lost fight.

As he was about to doze off, exhausted from worry, his ears perked up. From the tabletop by the window where the boys had left the shoebox, came a melodious, wailing sound.

A cricket song. Faint at first, then growing loud and insistent.

His eyes burning and barely squeaked open, Cu Bi dragged himself up and crawled over his brother, who didn't even stir, to get out from under the bed. He tottered toward the table.

"What's the matter with you, *dế ơi*—little cricket?" he whispered to the shoebox while suppressing a yawn. "Don't you like your sand bed and all that grass we put in for you?" The poor thing must be feeling lost and lonely, separated from the rest of his colony, Cu Bi thought. How much more scared it would be if it knew what his big brother had in store for it.

Scratching his nose in deliberation, he glanced back and forth between the shoebox and Cu Tí's bare feet sticking out from inside their makeshift shelter. Finally, as quietly as he could, he stood on his toes, unlatched the window shutters, and pushed them open.

Cu Bi took off the shoebox lid, grasped the box with both hands, and thrust it up against the windowsill. "Go on, cricket," he whispered urgently. "Here's your chance to fly away. I'm going to close my eyes and count to twenty. It's all up to you now."

He took his time and counted to thirty, just to be safe. Then he set the box back down and replaced the lid without peeking inside. After pulling the shutters closed, he slipped back under the bed, clambered over his sound asleep brother, and once again wedged himself snuggly between Cu Tí and the wall. Feeling secure and happier at last, he began dreaming at once.

The next morning Cu Bi awoke to a big commotion.

Cracking his eyes open, he caught sight of his big brother standing doubled over with his feet planted apart, glaring down at him from outside their cubbyhole.

"*What* happened?" demanded Cu Tí, his face flushed from hanging upside down. "What did you do? The cricket is gone!"

Even though still half asleep, Cu Bi almost let out a shout of joy and relief. The cricket had escaped—free and safe for now! It was all the young boy could do to hide the happy grin that threatened to break out on his face. He slowly rolled out onto the open floor, buying time.

"I didn't see anything. I swear," he mumbled groggily as he sat up and rubbed the sleep from his eyes. It was the honest truth; he wasn't lying. Still, he made sure he avoided Cu Tí's watchful gaze, but his heart was pounding so fast he was afraid his brother might hear it.

In a big huff, Cu Tí dropped down next to him, the open shoebox in his hands—empty.

He set it down on the floor between them. "We forgot to fasten the lid, so maybe he was able to squeeze out," he muttered, his face still scrunched up in disappointment. Then, clicking his tongue, "What a great cricket he was, too. Best of the bunch, the old man said so himself."

Cu Bi felt terrible, but he didn't know what to say.

"How about we save more money and get another one next Sunday?" Cu Tí proposed.

The younger boy crinkled his nose. "*Thôi*—nah. I want my own sweet rice. I was so hungry yesterday before lunch, my tummy made all sorts of weird noises."

"You're no fun at all," his brother declared, puffing and leaping to his feet.

Before he could dash off, Cu Bi wanted to know, "Can I keep the shoebox?"

"Whatever," replied Cu Tí, waving him off.

By the next day, Cu Tí had gotten over the missing cricket. He awoke to find, to his surprise, his little brother already up, kneeling on a chair at the table.

"What you doing there?" he asked.

"Hmm," said the younger boy.

Cu Tí crawled out on all fours and climbed on a chair next to his brother's. He knelt up and watched Cu Bi as the latter carefully tied down the lid on the shoebox with two big rubber bands.

"What you doing?" he repeated, leaning forward on his elbows.

"Fixing the lid so it stays on good," answered Cu Bi without looking up. "The box must be kept dark for Bé Xíu (Beh-Syu). Real dark."

Bé Xíu means "tiny baby" in Vietnamese.

The older boy waited a moment, then asked, "Who's Bé Xíu?"

"He's a baby dragon."

Cu Tí's eyes opened as big as his mouth. "There's a *dragon* in there?" he said, poking the box repeatedly with his finger.

Cu Bi whisked the box away from him, clutching it to his lap as he slid down in the chair. "You can't touch," he chided his big brother with a scowl. "He's asleep now."

Then he quickly added, "He sleeps all day long. He's a little baby."

Cu Tí stared at him suspiciously. "And how did Bé Xíu get here?"

The younger boy hesitated—mouth pouting, thoughts racing. "Umm . . ." he began while picking on the rubber bands, one after the other, "his Ba, Má came by and dropped him off in the box . . . while we were sleeping last night. That's right. And then—and then they had to leave right away. But they are coming back for him in a while."

His big brother urged him on with his probing gaze.

"There's lots of gunfire where they lived, see, just like at Tết," Cu Bi went on, increasingly fidgety in his seat. "Their house— they had a real nice house there—it was burned down. That's why his Ba, Má had to go back. They have to build a new house for all of them."

Cu Tí cocked his head, his eyes narrowing. "Bé Xíu told you all this?"

"Nah. He was too sleepy to talk," his brother said. "I—I just knew."

"Can I get a peek?" Cu Tí asked, as he stretched his whole body reaching for the box.

The younger boy twisted away, shielding the container with his arms.

"No, you can't," he squawked in alarm. "You're going to scare him." Then, in an appeasing tone, "I'll let you look later, when he gets a little bigger. Just don't bother him now."

Cu Tí hopped off his chair. "Whatever," he said haughtily. "I don't believe your story."

For the rest of the day, Cu Bi carried the shoebox with him wherever he went.

When Ba came home from work that evening, he found the boys anxiously waiting for him for dinner. Má had spent all day preparing a special meal in honor of the first anniversary of her father's passing. It consisted of asparagus soup, chicken with button mushrooms, and crispy roast pork, all in modest portions served on Má's finest dishware and laid out atop an altar table in the front room. Such a banquet was a rare treat and, for the boys, a much welcome break from their usual meager meals. Not least, it was a wonderful way to remember and honor Ông Ngoại, their beloved grandpa, who used to live with them and whom they dearly missed.

Ba lit a new candle and fresh incense, then the brothers followed their parents' lead as they all lined up facing the altar, put their hands together in front of their chests, bowed their heads, and said a silent prayer for the deceased. When they were done, Má moved the food to the dining table, and they sat down to eat, much to the boys' delight.

Noticing the shoebox next to Cu Bi's bowl on the table, Ba asked, "What's that you've got in that mysterious-looking box, Cu Bi?"

Before he could answer, his brother piped up: "A dragon, he said. But I don't believe him."

Má tapped Cu Tí on the back of his hand. "Now, now. Be nice to your little brother," she admonished. "Let him talk."

"I have a baby dragon in the box, *thiệt mà*—for real," Cu Bi said, glancing furiously at his older sibling. "His name is Bé Xíu. He just arrived last night."

"Ah," Ba sounded intrigued. "What does Bé Xíu look like?"

Cu Bi pointed at the decorated calendar on the wall, which depicted two dragons chasing a ball of fire under red-and-gold headlines with Vietnamese words and Chinese characters. "Like those," he said matter-of-factly. "But real teeny-weeny."

"With all the claws and tendrils, and the scaly body?" Má asked.

Cu Bi paused, his chopsticks frozen in mid-air. He seemed to think back, before answering with great seriousness, "Bé Xíu doesn't have all of those things yet. He's just a tiny baby now. His skin is really soft. And it burns easy. That's why I have to keep the box really dark for him."

Ba waited until the young boy had finished chewing a big piece of crispy roast pork. Then he turned to Má and wondered out loud, "Hmm. I'm not sure what we have around here that we can feed Bé Xíu. What do you think, Má?"

Cu Bi looked up from his bowl. "Don't worry," he declared with knowing confidence. "His Ba, Má left a lot of dragon food in the shoebox for him."

Ba smiled and tousled the boy's hair. "What a relief," he said. Then, catching Cu Tí eyeing the last few pieces of chicken and roast pork on the small plates, Ba laid down his chopsticks and rubbed his stomach. "Whew. I am full already. You boys eat up now. You want to grow big and tall, don't you?"

Over the following week, Cu Bi was seldom seen anywhere without his box, which he would allow no one to touch. He even surprised Má when he chose to stay home and guard his precious charge rather than join Cu Tí and other children in the neighborhood to play. But he would make a point of sharing with his big brother regular snippets of information about Bé Xíu's progress.

"He's staying awake a little more every day," he would reveal to the older boy.

And then, a little later on, "Bé Xíu really misses his Ba, Má. I heard him crying last night."

"I didn't hear a thing," retorted his brother, doing his best to feign total indifference.

"That's because you slept like a rock," Cu Bi said. "And you snored. Real loud, too."

Cu Tí rolled his eyes. "All right. When can I see him then?"

The younger boy pursed his lips as he tried to decide, before announcing, "Maybe soon. But you'll have to promise to play nice and not be rough with him." Sensing he had got his brother's attention, he dropped some more tidbits for good measure, "Bé Xíu is getting bigger and stronger all the time. Ô, and he's starting to grow purple scales on his skin now. They *shine* in the dark."

On Sunday afternoon Cu Tí rushed home from a neighbor kid's house, all agitated.

"Cu Bi. Where are you?" he shouted from the door. "You won't believe what I just heard."

He found his younger brother in the kitchen, the shoebox tucked under his arm. He was intently watching Ba refill the tank in the kerosene cooking stove.

"The cricket man, the cricket man," Cu Tí said between rushes of breath, sweat beading on his forehead. "Remember him? His village . . . there was big fighting. He was killed."

Ba stopped what he was doing and stood up straight, the kerosene container and the funnel still in his hands. He slowly set them down next to the stove. Many times in the past week, the boys had marveled to him about the old man at the market with his cage full of wonders.

Cu Bi stared at his brother in stunned silence. Had he heard wrong—or had Cu Tí?

The older boy went on, still gasping, "Me and Cu Bi . . . we didn't see him at the market this morning. But everybody has been talking about him, my friend Tuấn said."

Ba sighed and shook his head. "See how dangerous it is nowadays, boys?" he said. "It's the same everywhere, but even worse out in the countryside. This is the exact reason why I can't take you boys fishing, as much as I want to. Do you understand now?"

On occasion, the brothers had listened, enraptured, to Ba reminiscing about his childhood fishing trips with his own father. And they had been begging him ever since to take them to those same lakes and rivers, way outside the capital city, that he had enjoyed so much as a child.

But Cu Bi barely heard what Ba was saying. His mind was already skipping back to the old man who had sold him and his brother their first cricket just one week earlier: his thin, weathered hand that had so expertly scooped up their choice critter, his tired and gravelly voice instructing them how to care for it, the smell of mud and sweat on his black pajamas.

And then, suddenly, like a passing monsoon shower, the old man was gone—and with him, all those beautiful crickets, coal and fire alike. As though they had never existed, and the boys had never seen them around before. Where had they gone to, all of them?

Alongside his brother, Cu Bi nodded in answer to Ba's question. Of course, he understood what "danger" meant. It caused people and all kinds of things to disappear without a trace, like pencil drawings under an eraser. And it had surely kept him and his brother from learning how to catch fish using a skinny bamboo pole and live worms, as Ba used to do long ago, at their age.

Without thinking, the young boy clutched the shoebox tighter against his belly.

The brothers slept in late the next morning, making the most of those last days of summer before school started. Ba had gone to work, and Má gave each of the boys a bowl of leftover rice flavored with fish sauce and red peppers for breakfast. It was a far cry from their weekly treats of sweet rice on Sunday, but it was all the family could afford during the week.

Cu Tí noticed something odd immediately.

"Where's your shoebox?" he queried his little brother.

"I don't know," answered Cu Bi, half yawning. "But I don't need it anymore."

Má sat down next to him. "You don't? But what happened to Bé Xíu?"

"Ô, his Ba, Má came and got him last night," the young boy said, his mouth full. He paused to swallow, then went on, "Their new house is built. It's real quiet there, now. No more gunfire."

Cu Tí scowled in protest. "But I never got to see him. You never let me," he grumbled.

Eyes opened round, Cu Bi wiggled both hands to proclaim his innocence. "I didn't know his Ba, Má were coming. It was a surprise, I swear. And then—and then you were sleeping so sound I could not even wake you."

Má smiled and picked up the empty bowls from the table.

"Do you miss Bé Xíu?" she asked over her shoulders.

The young boy wrinkled his nose as he thought about it. "*Dạ có*," he finally said, nodding his head. "But I'm happy he is with his Ba, Má again. You know what he said to me, Má?"

"What, baby?"

"He said his Ba, Má are going to take him fishing as soon as they get home."

Cu Bi had no trouble at all picturing that wonderful fishing hole in the Land of Dragons— somewhere up there, above all the monsoon clouds. It would certainly have a creek full of fish flowing in the shadows of towering banyan trees and tall stands of bamboos, where one could sit and gaze at white herons rising from nearby rice fields—just as Ba had so longingly described. There would be no more bombing or fighting, only the soothing sounds of water and wind, and maybe of a flute attached to a soaring kite. It would be so quiet and peaceful one could just doze off. And there, dropping his line not very far downstream from Bé Xíu's family, would be the old man from the market with his cage full of chirping crickets. Because, Cu Bi could not help but wonder, maybe that is where people and crickets go after they die.

The thought filled his heart with warmth and lightness, the way it had felt that night when he had opened the box and let their fire cricket go.

Leaning on his elbows, with his face in his hands, the young boy grinned at his big brother.

"Want to go shoot marbles?" he said.

When Swallows Return

Last night she dreamed she was back on the lake. With him.

The water churned around them, frothy waves lapping at their rental motorboat. Above, storm clouds chased each other across the sky and covered up the last bit of sunlit blue. The wind picked up, whipping heavy raindrops against their faces. Thunder rolled in the distance.

The shoreline had vanished behind a rising mist, except for an island mound covered with evergreens looming in front of them.

"We better get to dry land quick," he said as he aimed the boat straight ahead.

They hurriedly put in on a strip of gravelly beach. He hopped out and dragged the boat from the roiling water. She rushed to

help him secure it to a scrawny aspen tree underneath a tall, sturdy white pine. Then, shrieking and laughing like children, they scrambled and ducked under a rocky overhang out of the pelting rain.

Soaked and shivering, she nestled in his arms, still laughing. They huddled on the ground on a mat of wet pine needles, leaning against the rock and each other.

He suddenly squeezed her shoulder and placed a finger on her cold lips. "Listen."

A tremulous sound glided across the water, its plaintive echo bouncing off the waves before dying down in the far reaches of the lake. "A loon," he whispered in her ear.

Listening for more cries, she asked, "Is it true that loons mate for life?"

"It's true if you believe it is." He turned to her, his eyes twinkling with tenderness. "I do."

Then, as she watched in stunned silence, her heart pounding so hard she could barely breathe, he knelt before her and took her trembling hands in his. Rain trickled down his face. A strange fire lit his eyes. His lips started to move when a sudden flash of lightning tore through the clouds and streaked across the black sky—

—and Kathy jolts awake.

A skinny ray of sunlight has snuck around the edge of the bedroom window curtain and landed on her pillow, waking her up.

Her pulse still racing and her body tingling with the warm glow of her disrupted dream, she rolls over and squeezes her eyes shut again, hoping desperately to resume the moment. But it's no use. The spell has been shattered and the moment is already flying away.

She can't remember the last time she dreamed of Joel, at least that she was able to recall afterward. That part of her life has seemed so far removed and shrouded in haze, mostly due to the decision she made long ago to stop dwelling in the past. Yet, to her astonishment—and yes, unabashed delight—the dream has unearthed such vivid details of that special summer day, as though the mist of half a century had suddenly lifted.

Kathy lets out a sigh. Grasping her pillow with both hands and burrowing her face in its soft folds, she feels a wave of pent-up memories washing over her.

It was another lifetime—the innocent early sixties whose sole remnants now are smiling portraits in faded colors or black and white that captured Kathy, then in her college years, with her dark brown hair in evolving styles, from a curled short cut to a bob with side bangs to a longer 'do with a part in the middle.

She met Joel in the summer of 1963 during a Beach Boys concert at the Prom Ballroom in St. Paul, Minnesota. The California Sound was all the rage, and the newly popular band had been playing one-night shows in various cities and towns throughout the Midwest. Kathy had gone with her best friend, Susie, and

Susie's resourceful beau, Tommy, who had managed to scrounge up last-minute tickets for the three of them.

The Prom was a madhouse that Friday night, its huge maple dance floor packed with boys and girls who had turned out in droves from all over the Twin Cities area to celebrate their new idols. Kathy recalled bumping into a group of Tommy's acquaintances, even dancing with some of them to the exultant music. But aside from a glimpse of the Boys performing on stage in their trademark striped shirts and white pants, her memory of the evening remained largely a blur of sound and motion, strangers' faces and hurried handshakes.

So she was taken aback when Susie called the next morning and asked, "Is it okay if I give your phone number to your latest admirer?"

"What admirer?" Kathy said. "What are you talking about?"

"Don't you play coy with me, girl." Kathy could almost see Susie wagging a finger at her. "It's Joey—Joel Bronstad. Tommy's friend from last night? I saw you kids slow-dancing to 'Surfer Girl' toward the end there. He's awfully cute. And he wants your phone number."

Kathy remembered the tall, slender guy with closed-cropped sandy hair and hazel eyes and his hands on her waist, but the music and the crowd had been so loud they could hardly exchange pleasantries, let alone carry on a conversation. Later, when the concert broke, they were separated in the chaotic shuffle out the door, and she had thought she would never hear from him again.

With a chuckle, she told Susie, "Sure. Why not?"

Joel rang up a few minutes later. They chatted for a while and connected so well over the phone she accepted his invitation to dinner that same evening—and the following weekend, and the weekend after that. By the time summer was over and they were heading back to college, he at the University of Minnesota in Minneapolis, and she at Winona State College, two hours' drive from the Twin Cities, Kathy recognized, not without some palpitation, that she and Joel seemed to have arrived at the threshold of something special.

That feeling intensified as he made the long commute to visit her every weekend he could. The clincher came when he showed up unannounced on her birthday that October, carrying two dozen red roses in his arm, with a sweet grin on his face.

"Surprise! I took a gamble you might stay in since it's the middle of midterm week," he said brightly as he handed her the flowers. "We've got to get you out, though, for a quick celebration at least." Then, with a teasing air of mystery, he added, "I have a little something else for the birthday girl, but let's wait until we get to the restaurant—your pick."

The "little something else" turned out to be a love poem that he had written in his own hand on fancy stationery slipped inside a birthday card. She blushed as she read it, feeling his intense gaze on her. The poem was rough around the edges, she thought, a little corny even. But hey, isn't anything heartfelt bound to be a little corny?

"It's . . . very nice. So sweet, really," Kathy sputtered after she finished reading, her cheeks burning as she reached for her sloe gin fizz without looking at him. "Is it by a poet I may know?"

His hand intercepted hers. "I hope you like it—even just a teensy bit?" he said, wincing in jest. "It'd sure break my heart if you didn't, though I can't say I'd blame you." Then his voice dropped to a melodramatic whisper. "It cost me a couple of nights' sleep, but I wrote it myself."

The expression on her face was such that Joel burst out laughing. "I know. What the heck does an engineering major know about poetry, right?" Then, winking at her, he went on with that earnest smile she had come to love, "But foolish me. I just figured if the Beach Boys could make beautiful music about a little deuce coupe, I should at least try to pen a poem for my girl."

Before Kathy could utter a word, he half-rose from his seat and leaned over across the table, took her face in his hands, and planted a tender kiss on her lips. The room full of young patrons their age burst into cheers and whistles as she blushed with embarrassed pleasure.

That was Joel, full of life and surprises. It never ceased to amaze Kathy that he had so many facets to him, all different and intriguing. A handy tinkerer, an avid sports fan and outdoorsman, a bon-vivant romantic and wannabe poet, and many other things as well, all of which she would discover in good time—all rolled into one terrific, lovable guy. It thus came as no real shock to her when she learned of his dream for the future during a moment of shared confidence.

"I've always wanted to be a U.S. Air Force test pilot," he revealed as they were discussing what they'd like to do after graduating from college, in less than two years for both.

"Why am I not surprised?" she chided him. "But what gave you the inspiration?"

"I'm from Little Falls, just up the road, where Charles Lindbergh had his childhood home," he said, his face suddenly animated. "So we all grew up worshipping this bigger-than-life legend, you know. And you can safely bet I wasn't the only hometown boy who dreamed of flying since he was knee-high to a grasshopper."

He then turned to her, a cryptic smile on his face. "Do you know that every one of the seven Mercury astronauts was a test pilot early in his career?" Watching her eyes open wide in reaction to his implied message, Joel grabbed her shoulders and playfully shook them. "Come on. We're in the space age now. One might as well shoot for the moon."

As she shared his joyful laughter, it dawned on Kathy she was in love with the boy dreamer.

During Christmas break that year, he invited her to spend a few days in Little Falls to meet his family and let him show her the home of his childhood hero. The next Easter, she brought him home with her to Rochester, Minnesota, and introduced him to her parents. In between the family visits, the two celebrated a white Valentine's weekend cooped up in her apartment in Winona, listening to albums by their new favorite group and daydreaming of California.

As summer 1964 rolled around, Joel suggested to her, "Can we make arrangements to wrap up our summer jobs before Labor Day weekend? I'd love to take you camping on Rainy Lake up north before we head back to school." He clicked his tongue with mock gravity. "Our last year as starving students, before we get booted out into the real world."

In later years, this trip has always been one of the first memories to pop into Kathy's mind whenever it starts wandering back to those early times, as it did in her dream last night. It was during a boat outing on their final day at Rainy Lake that they got caught in a summer storm and had to put in on a deserted island. There, down on his knee in the damp shelter under the outcrop, as a lost loon called to its mate out on the lake, Joel proposed to her.

Kathy had long suspected such a moment might come. Still, it took her breath away when it did, especially in that wild, wet setting. Soaked and trembling but smiling broadly through the rain that dripped down her face like rivulets of tears, she nodded her emphatic answer.

"Now, tell me honestly," said Joel as he stood and lifted her chin with a finger while staring in her eyes, "do you have any reservation about me wanting to become a pilot? What about your own plans? You've never shared much about them with me."

"I'll be a teacher. I can teach anywhere," came her quick reply.

His eyes grew narrower, more penetrating. "There'll be a lot of moving around, kiddo, to all kinds of different places. You'll be stuck with me alone, far away from your family and friends."

"I can imagine worse situations to be stuck in." Kathy laughed. "Look, I've never gotten up the courage to sign up for Peace Corps, as much as I've long dreamed of doing it. So maybe this will help make up for that? It will make me travel, see the world— force me out of my comfort zone."

He shook his head, dropped his brow against hers. "Boy, will it ever. You crazy, crazy girl."

They agreed they should wait until the next summer, after graduation, to get married. In the meantime, Joel could start inquiring about signing up with the USAF and the requirements for its pilot program. Huddled under the outcrop while around them sky and lake blurred into one gray sheet of rain, the excited couple began mapping out their future together.

The following nine months, their busy senior year, flew by. Before they realized it, summer 1965 was upon them, ushering in momentous changes—and a whole new life for both of them. They celebrated their graduations with a June wedding, a lovely, intimate affair with family and their closest friends, who after- ward saw them off to a two-week honeymoon in the sun and surf of Southern California. It was a glorious summer of fun and love, a perfect start to their married life with limitless possibilities ahead of them. The memories of those shimmery days have remained forever golden in Kathy's mind.

After they returned, the couple set out on the long road toward fulfilling Joel's dream. First, he applied himself to study- ing for the Air Force Qualifying Test, which he subsequently passed, using his own pun, "with flying colors." On the heels of it, he was required to report to Officer Training School in Texas in September 1965. Spouses were not allowed to come along, so the next three months proved trying for the newlyweds, who had to rely on letters and long-distance phone calls to keep in touch. It was Kathy's initial taste of separation as a young military wife, the first of many instances to surely come with their chosen life. The realization gave her pangs of mixed sadness and apprehension.

In December, Joel called home with big news.

"Are you ready, baby? We're on our way!" he shouted over the phone, almost stammering with excitement. "To the great adventure! I'll be home real soon for Christmas—to whisk you away with me right after the holidays." Then he started belting out "Fly Me to the Moon" in a squeaking, off-key imitation of Frank Sinatra that cracked Kathy up.

"Stop it," she pleaded between laughs. "I'm dying to hear what's going on."

She then learned with great pride and joy that he had graduated near the top of his training class. After rigorous screening tests, he had been selected to attend pilot school at Webb Air Force Base in West Texas. The Undergraduate Pilot Training was due to start in January 1966 and would last a little over a year. This time, however, Kathy would be allowed to accompany her husband and live with him as a true married couple in family housing on base.

In the years since, whenever she lets herself glance back on this eventful period of her life, it's always been with much fondness and nostalgia. 1966 was, in her heart, a "miraculous" year. Despite his grueling training schedule, she and Joel remained bright-eyed and very much in love, fully appreciative of their good fortune to be living their dream together. She met and made friends with other pilot wives and joined their support network to help each other adapt to their new environment. Off base, the wide-open space of West Texas beckoned—an exciting, brand-new world just waiting to be explored and discovered. Life was full and exhilarating, the first time Kathy truly felt in charge of her own destiny, shared with the one she loved.

Things were about to get even better, as a delightful surprise would soon interrupt the regular course of their life together and render it even more complete.

On their first wedding anniversary, which luckily fell on a weekend in June, Joel wanted to take her to Midland, a city four times as large as Big Spring, where the airbase was, to celebrate.

"Maybe we can do a little shopping there, before dinner," Kathy suggested. "I feel like I'm about to outgrow all my clothes."

"Anything your heart desires, my dear. But you sure look fantastic to me, as always." Joel snuck up from behind, gently wrapped his arms around her, and buried his face in the crook of her neck. "In fact, why don't you wear that same red dress I saw you in at the Beach Boys concert at the Prom, when we first met? Ah, what a sight for sore eyes you were that night. I'll never forget it for as long as I live."

Before she could reply, he swung her around, held her by the waist, and began swaying her in a slow dance around their tiny living room while softly humming "Surfer Girl" in her ear.

"It's no kidding, honey," Kathy whispered back to him, giggling. "I'm going to grow real *big* very soon. I really need to get some new clothes, and fast."

He began shushing her again—when at last something clicked in his mind and the humming stopped. The couple froze in their tracks, in the middle of the room. They stared at each other, his hazel eyes burning with questions, a half-scared, half-expectant look on his face.

Nodding to confirm the hunch that he still dared not voice, Kathy reached for his hand and placed it on her belly. As his lips slowly parted, wider by the moment, she burst out smiling, all jittery with excitement. "Are you hoping for a boy or a girl?" she asked, stroking his face.

Joel grabbed her by the waist with both hands and lifted her up in the air, almost bumping her head on the low ceiling as he let out a roaring "Yes!" Then, grimacing as if he just realized such enthusiasm might prove too rough for her new delicate state, he carefully set her down on her feet before covering her face with kisses.

"Hallelujah! What a perfect way to cap off an amazing year," he exclaimed, beaming from ear to ear. "I don't care if it's a boy or a girl. I just know it's going to be a perfect baby."

The timing couldn't have worked out more propitiously since the baby was due to arrive in early February the following year, right after Joel was to conclude his pilot training. Everything lined up like a dream, allowing the excited couple plenty of time to enjoy their blessing as well as prepare for the next phase in their married life. Or so it appeared.

As she entered the second trimester of her pregnancy, Kathy was hoping some of the early discomfort would soon taper off. Instead, she struggled even more and was eventually diagnosed with a complicated pregnancy, with worse unpleasantness predicted in the final stage. By late October, with three months to go, she was really showing, and the extra load on her small frame added to her difficulties. It became clear she would soon require more personal attention and care. Since Joel had just started the last phase of his training, which would demand much of his time and focus, the couple reluctantly agreed it would be best for Kathy to return to Rochester to await the delivery. There, in the comfort of her childhood home, her mother could keep a watchful eye on her while assisting with her daily routine.

In February 1967, immediately upon graduation from pilot school, Joel was granted leave and hurried to rejoin her, just in time to welcome the birth of their son, Michael. Both mother and child pulled through splendidly, and the young parents couldn't have been prouder or more elated. It was a tremendous time for them, a time of achievement and blessing. Kathy felt they had taken a giant stride forward into the future, which appeared to hold nothing but blissful promises.

On his second-to-last day of leave, Joel surprised her with a special gift. They were hovering over the crib in Kathy's bedroom, gazing in tireless wonder at their precious bundle in his sleep.

"This," Joel said as he placed a shiny piece of metal in her hand, "is half of my hard-earned graduation wings." He paused, cleared his throat before continuing. "I had them cut so that I can gift this half to my wife and my son, who are the whole world to me."

Kathy examined the small silvery object in her palm and felt a surge of emotions that she knew would be hard to control. "Why just half?" she asked lightheartedly while wiping her eyes.

"It's kind of a tradition with us new flyboys. To ward off bad luck, I was told. I'm hanging on to the other half, and the two pieces are not to be joined again. At least not until my funeral, which we hope won't be for a little while yet."

He pulled her close to him, resting her head on his shoulder. "I have not wanted to take time away from you and Michael to discuss this. But I did get my assignment, which I'll be reporting to, day after tomorrow," he said with a soft exhale. Then he held her more tightly, and his voice took on a brighter tone. "A fighter wing at England AFB in Louisiana. We did it, baby!"

Kathy understood just how competitive it was to get selected into the fighter track and what a great achievement this was for her husband. She hugged him and gave him a tender kiss.

"That's wonderful news, sweetheart," she said. "I'm really proud and happy for you. You've worked so hard and totally deserve it. Michael and I can't wait to join you down there."

To her puzzlement, he took her by the hand and guided her to sit down next to him on the edge of the bed. "That's what I want to talk to you about," he said, an uneasy smile on his face. "You see, England AFB is just temporary duty until I get fully trained on my new aircraft. My real assignment after that—it's nine months to a year at Biên-Hòa AFB in South Việt-Nam."

Up until then, Việt-Nam had seemed so far away to Kathy— a mysterious land in the tropics, covered in jungles, and rife with danger. She was generally aware that it had become the newest front line in the escalating Cold War. Young men had been drafted in droves and sent over there to fight the Communists and prevent them from taking over Southeast Asia, the same way they'd had to be stopped from overrunning the Korean Peninsula a decade earlier. The daily news had been inundated with unsettling reports and images of the bloody war. Yet, for whatever reason, perhaps as simple as wishful thinking on her part, it had never occurred to her that her husband might one day be called on to participate in that red-hot conflict.

His announcement stunned her. She could only stare at him, mouth agape, speechless.

Joel cupped her face in his hands and looked into her eyes. "I must go where my country needs me, you know that," he said, earnestly yet so disarmingly it was impossible to argue with him. "It's what I've been training for. I just wish it wasn't now. It's for sure the worst possible timing for us. I can't even stand the thought of being away from you and our baby."

He slid closer to her, and she breathed a long sigh and let herself fall back against him. She couldn't think of anything to say, struggling to keep her shock under control. As he wrapped his arms around her, she wished there was a way he could will her some of his strength.

"A year will zoom by fast. You'll see," Joel whispered in her ear, like a sweet promise. "You'll be so busy with little Michael, you won't even notice it." Then, catching his own words, he hid his face in her hair and let slip a groan. "Oh, damn! I'm going to totally miss out on Mikey's first year, aren't I?"

Closing her eyes, Kathy pulled her husband's arms tighter around her. All she wanted in that moment was to hang on to him with all her might, to the comforting warmth and feel of his body, which she had grown to know intimately—and never let go.

Joel left a couple of days later to report to England AFB in Louisiana. For the next several months, he underwent more intense training, not only on the new jet fighter he'd be piloting but also on jungle warfare in Việt-Nam. In June, his unit received orders to ship out within the month, and he was granted a thirty-day home leave. Fighting her own fear and anxiety, Kathy put on a brave front so that they could make the most of that precious time together, which also allowed Joel the only chance to truly enjoy his infant son. When he left for Việt-Nam in July 1967, Kathy made sure his wallet was stocked with family photos taken during those special days, innocent reminders of home to shield him from loneliness in the foreign land.

Meanwhile, powerful winds of change were sweeping across the nation, igniting civil rights and anti-war protests in cities and on college campuses. At the same time, out on the West Coast, the Summer of Love was in full swing, a rejection of conformist and materialistic values in favor of a simpler and more indulgent way of life. Alone at home in Minnesota with baby Michael, missing her husband and agonizing over his safety, Kathy watched the rapidly changing world with dazed eyes. She was seized with the unsettling feeling that a turbulent new era was already upon them. The cozy, complacent days had, overnight it seemed, been relegated to the past.

From Biên-Hoà, Joel made time out of his busy schedule to write home at least once a week. He always managed to sound cheerful, even amusing, no doubt for her and the family's benefit. The long-distance separation proved tougher than Kathy had imagined as she came to fully understand the horrific devastation as well as the gut-wrenching uncertainty of war. In just a short time after his departure, she went from religiously watching the TV news every evening to almost tuning it out altogether. And even though she tried her best to maintain a positive tone in her letters to Joel, she suspected that somehow he could sense her anguish from half the world away and was doing everything in his power to assuage it.

I got a surprise welcome the other day, he wrote shortly after arriving in country. *A friend of my big brother Jimmy, also a fellow hometowner by the name of Bob Olsen, stopped by my hooch to say Hi. As kids, I used to beg him and Jimmy to take me with them each time they snuck out to the Lindbergh home to play.*

Lots of fun memories we shared. Bob has been here since April, serving as one of the flight surgeons responsible for the base personnel's welfare. Small world, eh? We went down to the officers' club to catch up over a couple of beers (and lamented the fact they don't carry our local Hamm's brew around here). It was nice to see a familiar face in this remote corner of the world, and it made me think of home, how much I already miss it. But then again, sweetie, there isn't a thing I see every day that doesn't remind me of you and Mikey.

Joel made a point of never troubling her with details of his work, citing the secrecy of the operation he was part of. Nor did he allude to how dangerous the conditions were over there, which Kathy would just as soon not know anyway, having no control and feeling powerless over the situation. She was content to learn that the airbase served as a major logistical port and boasted the busiest runways in the world, and that it borrowed its name from the nearby small town, a sleepy, dirt-poor hamlet twenty miles northwest of Sài-Gòn, the capital.

Into that frantic environment, Joel seemed to settle without too much hassle, at least from what he let on in his regular notes home. This helped ease Kathy's mind to some extent.

In a letter dated a month after his arrival, he revealed more details of his new life:

Our workload is hectic but not unreasonable, and we rotate on weekend duty. On our free weekends, many of us venture out to the villages in the surrounding countryside to try and bring whatever relief we can to the locals: basic medical care, surplus

C-rations, material to shore up crumbling schoolhouses, etc. These poor souls live in such squalor it's hard to even describe, and every bit of help goes a long way in improving their lot. The children especially love us because we always show up bearing gifts of sweets—gum, chocolates, etc., which they absolutely crave (even those "John Wayne" bars, made extra hard so they won't melt in the tropical heat). Some of the villages are so remote we can only get there by helicopter or leaky sampan. I recall you once told me you had thought of joining the Peace Corps. Well then, eat your heart out, my dear. I'm now living your dream for you, and much more! But seriously, sweetheart, seeing how the folks here struggle to survive, even aside from all the fighting, makes me truly thankful for everything I'm blessed with: you, Michael, and the freedom we take so much for granted.

In time, Joel found out he had access on base to a communication system called MARS that employed short-wave carriers to patch a local phone line to one in the US. From then on, except during the busiest of times, he rarely missed signing up for allotted five-minute slots to call home to Kathy. Just to hear each other's voice, and for Joel, as he confided to her, to listen to Michael purring and babbling over the line static, was nothing short of a miracle. Bridging the miles and a vast ocean, this short-wave lifeline brought them all together. For five precious minutes twice a week, it helped them feel like a real family again.

By November 1967, they had more or less adapted to their separate new routines: Joel with his Air Commando Squadron at Biên-Hòa AFB, Kathy and baby Michael with her parents at their home in Rochester. Michael had by then grown into a miniature replica of his dad. At nine months old, he was curious and irrepressible, hell-bent on discovering the world on all fours as he crawled around with no fear and grabbed on to every piece of furniture to pull himself up. Laughing and chasing after her boy, Kathy finally let herself believe that Joel might be right after all: this year of separation would roll by fast enough, and he might even be home in time to hear Michael utter his first "Da-da."

Kathy tosses the pillow aside and rolls over into a curled-up position. Her stomach has started to churn, as it always does when her thoughts flit back to that November half a century ago. Prickly stings of anguish spread across her frail body, rendering her despondent and restive. Brushing loose strands of silver hair from her eyes, she runs her hands over her face to wipe away the tension, but to no avail. With a resigned moan, she lines the headboard with pillows and props herself up against them. Already her mind is being swept up in a torrent of long-banished memories—of that cold morning in late fall 1967.

It was about ten days out from Thanksgiving. Michael had fussed and cried throughout the night before, which was uncharacteristic of him, so Kathy put him down for an early nap after breakfast. His agitation had rubbed off on her, clouding her mood to match the somber sky and cold, dreary weather. But when the doorbell rang around mid-morning, it brought a smile to her face. It must be Bill, the thoughtful neighborhood mailman, who always delivered Joel's letters in person, right to the door, instead of just dropping them in the mailbox at the end of the driveway. He was well aware of Kathy's situation and, as a World War II veteran himself, surely understood how much the family looked forward to those letters from overseas.

But it wasn't the friendly postman at the door. Kathy's expectant smile faded into a silent "Oh" when she saw the two officers in dress blues standing erect on the stoop, their official Air Force vehicle parked at the curb.

Kathy knew in a flash.

Her breathing stopped. Gripping the doorknob with both hands, she turned around to call for her mother—an instinctive cry for help—but no sound escaped. The abrupt movement sent the hallway spinning around her, and her hands slipped off the knob. Fortunately, her mother, who had followed her to the door, was right behind her to break the fall. The two officers rushed to give a hand. They carried her to the davenport in the living room.

The next thing Kathy knew, she was half reclined on the davenport, her limp body drooping against her mother's. Her head was swimming and she felt queasy, as though she were bobbing on rough waters. Her temples pulsed painfully with each thudding heartbeat. She was chilled all over, shivering and perspiring at the same time in her sweater. All of her senses were heightened even as she seemed strangely detached from the scene—a mere bystander watching a nightmare unfold around her in disjointed slow motion.

The officers respectfully remained on their feet, caps in hands and solemn-faced, as one of them broke the news to Kathy in a grave monotone. Staring blankly ahead, she heard every word the man said. How Joel's airplane had been struck by anti-aircraft artillery during a night mission and exploded over Việt-Cộng–controlled territory, an area known as the Parrot's Beak along the Cambodian border. And how Search and Rescue had rushed to the spot at first daylight but had not been successful in recovering any remains. Next to her, she felt her mother's body heaving with quiet sobs, her damp hands gripping Kathy's own.

The other officer was a chaplain, and he offered to say a prayer with them. Her mother must have nodded consent because the chaplain's voice droned on, measured and consoling. As it did, Kathy's mind began to float away. Images scrolled by before her eyes like on a reel of film, a live album of Joel and her at various moments in their journey together. Big and small, poignant and lighthearted moments. All laced with the joys or the occasional heartaches of the love she had counted on to fill their whole lifetimes. Slowly awakening to the inexorable reality, she felt her heart throb with unbearable pain—and the tears finally burst free.

Kathy's memory of the rest of that morning and of the following days and weeks remains fuzzy at best, forever cloaked in the cold grayness of grief and despair. She vaguely remembers fighting through the fog just to be able to get out of bed and go through the motions each day. Thankfully, her family and Joel's were right by her side to lend their support and help her navigate through that horrendous patch, one torturous day and sleepless night at a time.

Like festering wounds, habits—even recent ones—lingered. For a while, Kathy would catch herself still keeping an ear out for the phone at those regular hours when Joel used to call home, praying to hear the bell she knew would never ring again, then dying a little when it did not. The hardest blow, however, came the week after Thanksgiving when a care package she had mailed to Joel earlier was returned unopened from Việt-Nam. It was a holiday gift box lovingly packed with some of her husband's favorite treats: his mom's pecan oatmeal cookies and *lefse* flatbread, and Kathy's homemade rhubarb jam. The shock and pain at the sight of the returned package felt just as sharp as on the day she had received the news, plunging her into a deeper depression.

In the end, it was little towheaded Michael who achieved what none of his adult relatives could. With his boundless energy and irresistible grin, he never quit clamoring for his mother's love and attention and thus succeeded, a little each day, in pulling her out from the darkness she had sunk into. Clutching her hand for support and refusing to let go, he insisted on making her his partner in all his exploring adventures. And so, step by teetering step, alongside her eager boy, Kathy emerged back into the world of the living.

Weeks stretched into months, and then months into a year. When, before his second birthday, Michael was hospitalized with a serious respiratory infection and required vigilant care around the clock, Kathy was jolted into acknowledging what she had known all along—that she needed all her focus and energy to maintain control of both their lives. Sitting at her boy's bedside, watching his little body fight for every breath, she made a tearful pledge that from then on, she would devote herself entirely to his welfare and to building a good life for them both, even on her own. It was time to set aside sorrow, anger, and self-pity, to put the past firmly behind her and bury its ghosts once and for all.

And buried they had remained all these years, seemingly laid to rest under the dust of time. It had required no small amount of self-discipline on her part, but the effort had helped her find solace and purpose in all her kids: her own son as well as the generations of children whom she had taught over the years in her elementary school classrooms. Never had she suspected that one phone call out of the blue could shatter that hard-earned peace and upend her sedate existence. Yet that was exactly what had happened less than twenty-four hours ago.

Kathy takes a deep breath and wearily shakes her head to chase the crowded thoughts from her mind. She glances at the alarm clock on the nightstand. It's only seven o'clock. Her visitor is not expected until ten, as he has to drive to Rochester from Eau Claire,

Wisconsin. But Kathy has been on pins and needles awaiting his arrival since the curious phone call yesterday afternoon.

It was a man's voice, not all that young but not quite old either, that greeted her on the other end when she picked up the phone to answer. His peculiar query immediately got her attention.

"May I please speak to Mrs. Katherine Bronstad . . . Lieutenant Joel Bronstad's widow?"

It had been nearly half a century since anyone outside of the family had mentioned Joel's name, let alone his official USAF rank. It took her a couple of seconds to find her words.

"This is she. Who is this, and how can I help you?"

The voice grew softer, with a hint of relief. "Please forgive the rude intrusion, ma'am," it said. "I'm so glad to be speaking with you. My name is Danny Winkler. Lieutenant Bronstad and my late father, Captain Winkler, served together at Biên-Hòa Air Force Base in South Việt-Nam during the war. I was going through some old boxes, and I believe I found something here that belongs to you."

The man went on to explain that he had in his possession an old sealed envelope addressed to Kathy, which he would be happy to drive down from Eau Claire, where he was calling from, and deliver in person to her. He had been able to track down her unlisted phone number with the help of the Department of Veterans Affairs and would like to verify that her address was still the same as the one inscribed on the envelope.

Kathy held her breath. "Did you see who the letter was from?"

"I'm not positive, ma'am. There's no return address on it, just some scribbled note," Danny said. "I realize all this must be a big surprise to you, to say the least, and awfully confusing. But it might help if I could explain everything face to face. Would it be all right with you if I come down tomorrow, say, at ten in the morning?"

After mumbling her agreement and confirming that the man indeed had the correct address, Kathy hung up in a daze. She dropped down in a nearby chair, her hands still shaking. What had just happened? She wasn't quite sure. Ever since that horrible morning in November 1967, Kathy had developed a strong distaste for, if not outright fear of, surprises. This one, in particular, rattled her nerves. It was the first time in decades that she had heard Joel's name brought up in the same sentence as Biên-Hòa and Việt-Nam. By a total stranger no less, albeit one whose personal history appeared to have intersected with her own. All through the evening and night, Kathy's mind was caught in a time-warped merry-go-round, churning over memories and emotions she had long thought, if not forgotten, then safely locked away.

This morning, as she struggles to pull herself together in the last moments before the visitor arrives, Kathy begins to wonder what fragment of the past is about to get unearthed after all these years, and how it may rip open old wounds. Apprehension steals over her.

By nine thirty, Kathy is sitting on the davenport in the living room, her hands folded in her lap, nervously awaiting the arrival

anything." He looks at her with kind, trusting eyes that convey much more than his words—a spontaneous kinship born of shared adversity. "Sadly, they're all gone now. Mother was the last to pass on, just over a month ago."

"Oh, Danny." Kathy's heart goes out to him. "I'm terribly sorry for your loss." Were it not for the fact they've barely just met, she would reach out for his hand in comfort.

He shakes his head, a wistful expression on his face. "Thank you, ma'am. I really miss her. But, you know, Mother was never blessed with robust health, so I was quite grateful she had a peaceful end rather than a long, drawn-out struggle." He clears his throat then sits up straight, his hands clasped in front of him. "Sorry for rambling on. What I really came to tell you, ma'am, is that I'd been sorting through Mother's things and I ran across this large box in the back of her closet that contained all kinds of personal items of my dad's from Việt-Nam. Graves Registration must have boxed them up and shipped them to Mother right after he died. Anyway, among those was a hardcover copy of *The Green Berets*, and by pure chance, I was flipping through the book when I found this, tucked in the back behind the cover."

Danny reaches into the inside pocket of his sport coat, pulls out an envelope, and hands it to Kathy. It's an old-fashioned Via Air Mail envelope with a red-white-and-blue trim all around the border. Inscribed on the front in bold print are her name—Katherine Bronstad—and address. With a jolt that sets her heart pounding, Kathy recognizes Joel's handwriting, which she used to know intimately from all his letters home. The envelope is sealed and feels somewhat lumpy, as if it might contain more than just paper. There's no return address, but scribbled in the lower right corner is a faint pencil annotation that Kathy can just barely make out. In unfamiliar handwriting, it reads, "To mail to Joel B's wife. In case."

Kathy looks up in disbelief. "This was addressed to me by my husband. But how . . .?"

"I can only guess that the penciled writing was my dad's, but I have no idea how the letter came into his possession," Danny says. "After I found it in the back of his book, I did some digging around and called a bunch of numbers at the VA and the USAF. I was able to confirm that there was a Lieutenant Joel Bronstad who served at Biên-Hòa in 1967 in the same squadron as my dad. The records showed he was killed in action only days before my dad, and you were listed as his next-of-kin and survivor. I'm just glad you haven't changed your name or moved away so that I'm able to bring you the letter today."

"How incredible is that," Kathy says, smiling pensively. "And maybe in the nick of time, too. My son Michael works out of state and worries about me living alone, so he's been bending my ear about selling the house and moving to an assisted-living facility."

She asks Danny about his family, and they visit some more. After a while, he stands up.

"I've got another appointment to run to, so I best be on my way," he says apologetically. "But I'd like to leave my number with you in case you think of any questions or just wish to talk." He hands her his business card. "Please call anytime. It'll be a pleasure to hear from you."

"Can I give you a hug, Danny?" Kathy says. He bends down and she puts her arms around him, patting affectionately on his back. "It's awfully nice of you to travel all this way to deliver my husband's letter in person. It means the world to me. I can't thank you enough. Truly."

"I'm just sorry it was misplaced all these years," Danny says, a slight catch in his voice. "No one even knew the letter existed. I'm sure Mother didn't, or she would have done the same thing for you. But I'm happy it's finally in your hands, as intended."

After seeing him to the door, Kathy returns to the quiet living room and sags down on the davenport, drained. The long-errant letter lies face-up on the coffee table as if just delivered in person by Bill, the thoughtful neighborhood postman of years past. For a moment, she simply sits and gazes at Joel's handwriting, strong and beckoning despite the faded ink. And then, as was her habit back in those days each time she received mail from him, she tries to picture her husband propped up on his cot in his hooch before lights-out, writing under a dangling light bulb. And her heart swells with loving tenderness, as it always did on such occasions.

Kathy retrieves a letter opener from the end table's drawer and slits open the envelope. As she pulls out a thin sheaf of pages, a small, flat object wrapped in paper bound with Scotch tape spills out on the coffee table. She picks it up and turns it over in her hand, feeling its jagged hardness under the wrap paper, then decides to set it aside for now. Pausing to compose herself, she slips on her reading glasses, unfolds the letter, and settles back in her seat.

Biên-Hòa AFB, 12 Nov 1967, 1600 hours

> *My dear, sweet Kathy,*
>
> *All day today, my head has been filled with thoughts of you and Mikey, and it really hits home just how much I've been missing you both. How I long for that happiest day not too far off when I can smother both of you in my arms and press you close to my heart and never let go. Of course, I do think of you guys every day, but today is different because you've been on my mind nonstop since I started awake before first light this morning. It might have been the rain on the hooch's tin roof that woke me up, a remnant shower of the outgoing monsoon season. There was something about the steady drumming of rain in the dark that stirred up such longing in me for home and family, so I just lay awake until daybreak, hugging you and our boy in my thoughts.*
>
> *Normally, once I get going with my daily routine, I easily lose myself in it, but not so today. That feeling of homesickness just stuck with me and followed me around, and no matter what I was doing, my mind kept darting back to the two most important people in my life. So after the briefing and flight planning for the evening sortie, I stopped by the dispensary to look in on my former neighbor,*

Bob Olsen, who is also our flight surgeon. I believe I mentioned him to you in an earlier letter. He happened to be in between patients and welcomed the chance to visit for a little while. Bob quickly picked up on my restlessness and wanted to prescribe a crew rest, but I didn't think it was warranted, so we just shot the breeze and caught up on each other's family. I showed him my wallet pictures of you and Mikey, and he was excited to share that he and his wife Nancy are expecting their first child any day now. Our visit, quick as it was, did help to clear my head and lift my spirits. Then as I got back to my hooch, it finally dawned on me what else had been troubling me, aside from missing you both.

Oh, sweetheart, it's tough enough that we're an ocean apart from each other, so I can only imagine how much harder it must be for you as a young mother alone with her first baby. I've been trying my best to set your mind at ease and shield you from unnecessary worries, but what I'm about to say may upset you. That's the reason I never broached the subject before and am writing this letter instead, which by the way shall be mailed out only in case something should happen to me. You'll understand why in just a minute.

You know I'm happy and proud to serve our country, but there's no denying the real danger involved. We're at war after all, no matter what the politicians say, and the Việt-Cộng are armed with the latest anti-aircraft from their Soviet and Red Chinese allies. Every time we take off from the base on a mission, the likelihood of some of us not coming back is a reality we all must face. God *knows I've been to enough "Glad to Be Alive" parties to celebrate a comrade's escape from a close call, who could just as well not have made it. All I can do is keep my head and carry out my job the best way I know how and just hope that my number isn't up any time soon. But honey, <u>IF</u> and when that day should come, I would want one last chance to say these words to you:*

You're the best thing that has happened to me, and I love you with all my heart. I obviously wish we could spend a whole lifetime together as we vowed to, but I bear no bitter regret and am grateful for every moment we've shared. Thank you, my darling Surfer Girl, for your love and all you've given me and for making my days on earth a life well-lived. Promise me you will go on and live <u>your</u> life to the fullest, for you deserve all the happiness there is to have. Please tell Mikey for me, when he's big enough to understand, how much Daddy loves him and is proud of him, how I miss not being around to watch my boy grow up and be a part of his life. The mere thought of it breaks my heart, and my only consolation is in know-ing that you will love him plenty enough for both of us. He is very lucky to have you as his mom.

I'm including with this letter the other half of my graduation wings, to be paired up with the half I left with you. Whenever you and Mikey look at these wings, just remember you were never far from my thoughts, even while I was up among the clouds. Also included, you'll find a "poem" (if I dare call it that) that's been milling around in my head and that I've finally just put down on paper. It's from me to you, and I hope it brings you love and comfort in your times of loneliness. It's no doubt clumsy and a little corny like the stuff I used to pen for you when we first met—a lifetime ago, it now seems. But now, as then, my sweet, I meant every word I wrote.

And although no words can express all my love for you and Mikey, I feel my heart lightened for having had this chance to say goodbye—<u>just in case.</u> I'll drop this note and everything else in a sealed envelope addressed to you, which I will entrust to the hands of my brother-in-arms and hooch mate, Captain "John Wayne" Winkler, a real nice fellow Midwesterner from Wisconsin. He'll hold on to it for me and will mail it out <u>if and ONLY if</u> something should happen to me.

I pray to God you never have to read this letter.

It's now time I get down to the flight line to prepare for our evening sortie. Here's a hug as big as the sky for you and Mikey. I live for the day when I can hold you again for real. That's my goal and guiding light, the one thing that's keeping me sane and focused amid all this madness.

All my love always,
Your husband Joey

Kathy's hand drops to her side, still gripping the letter. Her shoulders shake as Joel's words echo through her mind. Fifty years it has taken for them to reach her because a twist of fate had sent both him and his hooch mate to their untimely deaths within days of each other, such that the letter never got mailed.

But the words still ring vibrant and urgent, as if Joel himself had just whispered them in her ear, his comforting arms wrapped around her. She can feel the sense of foreboding weighing on her husband's mind on what turned out to be his last day on this earth, but it was totally like him to not let anything deter him from his mission.

Kathy removes her glasses and wipes her eyes with a handkerchief. The tears keep coming, but not in big drops—just a soft dew damping her wrinkled cheeks. Breathing so faintly her body hardly stirs, she sits immobile in the late morning stillness and lets her thoughts quiet down. Then, blinking away the lingering mist, she puts her glasses back on and picks up the last page.

To my wife Kathy and my son Michael, with all my love

When I'm Gone

In the spring
When swallows return to the old churchyard
And pear trees are white with blossoms
I will be there each morning
Bright sunshine on your windows
And in your heart

As summer arrives
With bursting colors and endless days
In the warm breeze that rustles your daydreams
You will hear my voice
Whispering your name

When the leaves turn golden
In the brisk autumn air
And soft clouds trail across the open blue
I will sprinkle along your walk
Pine needles and sweet memories
Fragrance of yesteryears

On long, cold winter nights
When your heart wonders
As you sit alone by the fireplace
Rest your weary eyes and listen to the rain
Singing you my soul's lullabies

Kathy presses the poem to her chest so that the tears won't stain it.

She had cherished every sweet little poem Joel had penned for her over the years, but this one touches her like no other. It's quintessential Joel, whimsical yet tender, but it also bares his unreserved love and longing for her and Michael during his final hours, when the prospect of tragedy was looming large in his mind. His anguish and loneliness breathed through the page, as also evidenced by the frantic scribble. Yet his last thoughts had been to comfort her and their son. Clutching the letter with both hands, she yearns for Joel with all her heart as she did in the days and weeks and months that followed his death—so much it hurts.

Through the haze of time, Kathy sees her husband in his flight suit grinning from ear to ear as he proudly posed in front of an aircraft with a raised cockpit. It was an old fighter plane used in pilot training, but it still made an impressive backdrop to her favorite photograph of him, the one she snapped herself not long after their arrival at Webb Air Force Base. How young he was then, handsome and eager and brimming with confidence. How she loved him and longed to share his life with him, wherever it might lead them. So much happiness and excitement lay ahead of them, the future as wide open and bright as his beloved sky.

They all come flooding back to her now, those ardent emotions of her youth, long since put out but now rekindled to a blaze by Joel's devoted last words. His untimely death bored an indelible void in her heart, and Kathy has never felt the same about any other man. Even though life after Joel was a hard struggle, especially in the early years, there has never been a flicker of doubt in her mind that she would have taken the same journey with him all over again.

Kathy unwraps the small packet bound with Scotch tape and retrieves the missing half of her husband's graduation wings. Its original shine has been dulled and mottled with time, but it looks a perfect match to the half Joel had given her before he departed for Việt-Nam. When, after his death, his personal effects were returned to her from Biên-Hòa, she did go through all the boxes but couldn't find the missing wing and simply assumed it lost in the shuffle. Here it is now, in the palm of her hand all these years later, the final gift from Joel—a small piece of himself. At long last, the broken wings can be put back together and the complete set passed on to Michael. Kathy runs her fingers over the wing's jagged edges, raises it to her lips, and kisses it, long and tender. Eyes closed, she feels her husband's loving embrace around her, his warm breath on her neck as he murmured in her ear, *For my wife and my son, who are the whole world to me.*

All these past decades, Kathy has stayed put in this dated Craftsman home where she and Joel had last known happiness together, never wishing to move. It is as if, she now realizes, on some subconscious level she has never quite accepted the loss of her husband and is still waiting for his return. Now suddenly, out of the past, by nothing short of a miracle, he has indeed come back to her. For one last farewell.

Head bowed, Kathy remains motionless, immersed in nostalgia. As the memories gradually release their grip, she gathers her thoughts for another moment before rising from the davenport. Gently shaking the stiffness from her limbs, she moves over by the armchair, picks up the telephone on the end table, and dials.

It takes several rings on the other end before Michael's voice answers: "Hello?"

"Hi, darling. It's me. Are you free to talk?"

"Hey, Mom," he says, an anxious note in his voice. "Are you all right?"

"Oh, I'm fine. How are you? How are Lisa and the kids?"

"We're all doing good, thanks. The kids miss you." A hesitation, and then, "Mom, have you given some thought to what we discussed the last time?"

"About the assisted living? Honey, you know this old house is where I grew up, and you too. It's not an easy decision to just up and leave it. . . ."

"I understand, Mom. I really do. It's my childhood home, too, as you just said. But I love you, and I worry about you. You've been having dizzy spells; plus, you're forgetting things—"

"Michael—"

"—and I'm a four-hour drive from you. I just can't get to you fast enough in case you need me. I wake up at night wondering how you're doing."

"Oh honey, you shouldn't have to. But I appreciate your concern and I love you all the more for it. That's why I called: to tell you—I think I may just be ready for the change."

There's sudden silence on the other end.

"You see, it's the memories in this house I've been hanging on to. A whole lifetime of them. Why, the most important events in my life all took place right here: my childhood; my wedding; you, of course; the day I got the news of your dad—"

"Mom—"

"It's okay, Michael. Let me finish. Your grandparents also lived in this house until the very end. And so, I'm surrounded here with memories of all the people I love. The simple truth about memories, though, is that they're so much more than just objects or places, you know? It's really what remains in our hearts long after our loved ones are gone." Kathy chuckles softly. "I'm sorry. Here I go, just babbling on. What I'm trying to say is quite simple: I've decided I actually don't need to stay in this house to have my memories. I will take them with me wherever I go."

It's a moment before Michael speaks up, his voice quiet and thoughtful. "Mom, you do know I only want what's best for you. . . ."

"I know, baby. And I want to set your mind at ease. It's time."

He clears his throat. "We can discuss all the options whenever you feel comfortable. Including you coming to live with us, which you've kept saying no to. But now, if you're up for company next weekend, we'd love to drive up to see you. The kids will be thrilled. They really miss their Granny." He pauses before adding, "I miss you, too, Mom."

"I miss you, darling," Kathy says, turning Joel's graduation wing in her free hand. "It will be wonderful to see all of you. By the way, there's some mail and a packet that just arrived for you this morning. It'll all be set aside, waiting for you when you come."

"You know who it's from?"

Kathy smiles. "From someone very special and dear to us both. But I really must tell you in person. I'll see you soon, honey."

After hanging up, Kathy sits back on the davenport and stares out the window. The storm front must have passed through because the late summer sun is bursting out again, splashing a brilliant rainbow of light upon the glass. The sight of it fills her with contentment and quietude, as she hasn't felt in quite some time. Softly, she reads out her husband's poem again:

In the spring
When swallows return to the old churchyard
And pear trees are white with blossoms
I will be there each morning
Bright sunshine on your windows
And in your heart . . .

Spring may have been long gone, but in Kathy's heart, the swallows have only just returned.

A Cup of Love

"Thanks for letting us drop Kimmie off tonight, Mom," says the woman, who looks in her late thirties or early forties, as she entrusts the little girl to the older woman standing across the open threshold. Then, carefully so as not to wrinkle the elegant dinner gown, she bends down and kisses the child on her rosy lips. "Umm-muah. Mommy and Daddy will be back soon. Let *Bà Ngoại*—Grandma—know if you need anything, okay? Love you, honey."

Five-year-old Kimmie nods and waves goodbye with the ragdoll in her hand, jiggling the pink bow in her bobbed black hair, her other hand securely nestled in her grandmother's.

"You guys enjoy the reception," Grandma says to Mommy as she's hurrying back to the car waiting at curbside. "Kimmie and I will have a great time with each other."

Closing the door behind them, the gray-haired woman leads her granddaughter by the hand down the entrance hallway, through the quiet living room, and into a bright, airy kitchen. At near seventy, Grandma still carries her delicate petite frame with easy grace, even if her gait appears slightly hampered by invisible aches and pains.

"My, my, aren't you pretty tonight," she says, hugging Kimmie close to her. "Look at those lovely flowers on your dress. What are they, springtime daisies? But you know, sweetheart, you are even prettier than all the flowers combined."

The little girl smiles broadly, revealing a pair of cute dimples and some missing front teeth. She stretches her tiny arms around her grandmother and burrows her face in the folds of the old woman's silk blouse. "Where is *Ông Ngoại*?" she asks.

"Mr. Peterson next door is showing Grandpa his new truck," Grandma says. "He'll be real pleased to see you when he gets back. It won't be long." She pulls out a chair at the kitchen table and places a booster cushion on it. "Let me help you up here. There you go. . . . And how about we sit your baby doll right across from you on top of the table? That way you can watch her at all times, yes? Mommy said you already ate dinner, so do you want to share some *bánh đậu xanh* dessert with *Bà Ngoại* now? Or is your little tummy too full still?"

"What's that, *bánh* . . .?"

"*Bánh đậu xanh.* Ah, why don't I just show you?" Grandma retrieves a packet from the cupboard, unfolds the red Saran wrap around it, and pours yellow squares of cookies out onto a plate.

"It's mung bean cookies," she explains. "They are powdery soft, and so yummy. One of my favorite treats ever since I was a little kid like you. Do you want to try one?"

Kimmie crinkles her nose. "May I have milk with it?"

"Of course, you may," says Grandma with a smile. "But I'll have mine with hot tea."

She starts the jasmine tea brewing, then gets Kimmie her paper plate and plastic fork in Christmas colors, along with a small glass of milk. When the tea is ready, Grandma pours herself a cup before sitting down next to the child. With her fork, she picks up a mung bean square and nimbly drops it on Kimmie's plate.

"Now, take a small piece and put it in your mouth. Go on," Grandma says, giving the little girl enough time to follow through. "But don't chew. Just let it melt on your tongue. Yes, like that. . . . Mmm-mmm. Isn't it delicious? I have got to have some myself."

Kimmie nods and giggles and draws a big gulp from her glass of milk. Grandma helps herself to a cookie, tastes a morsel of it, then lifts the cup to her lips with both hands, pausing briefly to inhale the fresh fragrance before taking a sip. The child watches her with unblinking eyes like black opals.

"*Bà Ngoại ơi*," Kimmie says, "why do you always drink tea in that cup?"

"How clever of you to notice, sweetie," answers Grandma as she sets the cup down. Then, leaning over with a napkin, she gently wipes a trace of milk from the child's upper lip. "This teacup was a special gift to me," she continues. "I've had it for a long time now, and I've always liked it a lot . . . maybe as much as you like your baby doll or your bunny blankie."

It's a small alabaster cup, the size they normally serve at Chinese restaurants, and quite ordinary-looking except for its light shade of flesh tone, with dark red veins showing through.

The little girl stares at it, puzzled. "But it is not pretty like Dolly," she says.

Grandma chuckles and plants a kiss on her hair. "Do you want to hear a story?"

"Please, please, *Bà Ngoại*," Kimmie cries and claps her hands. "Tell me a story!"

Grandma slips an arm around her granddaughter and nudges her closer, cradling the little head against her shoulder. "Are you ready?" she whispers in Kimmie's ear.

The child nods eagerly, her eyes round with anticipation.

"Long, long ago, when I was a little girl just like you, I lived with my parents and my baby brother in a far-away land called Việt-Nam. It was sunny and hot all year round where we lived, and it rained a great deal, too. There was also a war rumbling on—you know, soldiers fighting each other, gunshots popping like firecrackers, and explosions as loud as thunder, especially at night. My brother and I used to be scared when it came time to go to bed, so our mother would come in and tell us stories until we both fell asleep. I still remember one particular story that I liked above all others. I hope you will like it as much as I did.

"Now, this is an old legend that goes way back, to a time so early it seems shrouded in fog. So I'm going to ask you to close your eyes, sweetheart, and then try to imagine a world that was brand new and covered with blue mountains and green forests, with a white-water river running through it and people living in small villages along the riverbanks. . . . Can you see it yet?"

Grandma watches with a tender smile as Kimmie's eyes flutter shut, and her hands ball up in small fists of concentration. Nodding excitedly in answer to her grandmother, the little girl snuggles against her warmth, drinking in every word from her soft, gravelly voice.

"The people there were ruled by a king, who was wise and kind and loved by all. King Hùng lived with his family in a castle with high towers overlooking the river. His wife, the queen, had died early and left him to care for their children. The youngest among them was a little princess whose name was almost as pretty as yours: Mỵ-Nương. The king and the nice folks who helped look after the orphan princess all adored her, and together they did everything they could to keep her from being lonely and sad. As the years passed, the little princess grew into a young woman as lovely as springtime and cherished by all the people around her.

"Mỵ-Nương's favorite place in the whole castle was her room at the top of a high tower. There, many an evening at the end of a hot day, she sat by the window and watched the setting sun sparkle over the water like gold. As she gazed at the birds flying up the river to return to the forests, the young princess dreamed of places she had never been. And then, one evening, a cool breeze wafted in the window and carried to her ears a melodious sound from the river below. It danced and wrapped around her like a ribbon of silk, the prettiest sound she had ever heard, and it filled her heart with happiness. Every sunset from then on, My-Nương waited by her window for the mysterious sound, and it kept coming back to her like a loyal friend."

Kimmie stirs and twists, her eyes now open, trying to catch Grandma's. "*Bà Ngoại ơi,*" she says, unable to hold back any longer, "what makes that sound? Is it like your music box?"

Grandma caresses the little girl's hair. "What a wonderful quick mind you have, honey. Bear with me for just a minute, and we'll find out together. As I was saying, every evening the princess would look forward to the beautiful sound that she had come to enjoy so much. Until one night, it went silent. The sound never came. Nor did it return the next night, or the one after that. After several quiet evenings, the young princess fell ill. She lost her appetite and just tossed and turned all night long. In time, she grew so weak she seldom left her room in the tower anymore. Meanwhile, none of the potions prepared by the wisest men at the court seemed to help My-Nương. Her condition worsened with each day. At long last, not knowing what else to do, a lady who waited on the princess got up the courage and stepped forward to tell the king about the mysterious sound at sunset. King Hùng, who had been desperately worried, immediately sent his guards out to the villages to track down its source.

"It wasn't long before the royal guards hurried back with exciting news: they had discovered where the unknown sound had come from. There was this young fisherman from a poor village up the river, the king was told. His name was Trương-Chi, and he lived with his old father in a straw hut by the water's edge. Every morning, Trương-Chi would sail his small boat downstream where he cast his fishing net, only to head home at sundown. It was said that the fisherman was an excellent player of the flute, and that he often would play it while sailing home after a long, hard day of work. The evening wind would carry the beautiful sound far and wide throughout the green valley, and his music brought joy to the poor villagers."

Kimmie begins to stir again, so Grandma gives her shoulder an affectionate squeeze. "Yes, sweetie," she says with a loving smile. "You're itching to know what a flute is, aren't you? It's a musical instrument made of a hollow stick of bamboo with a row of holes on the top. By blowing into it while moving your fingers over the holes, you can produce a wide range of musical notes. Of course, it would take a lot of practice and talent to get really good at it, and it appeared the young fisherman had plenty of both. But it so happened that he had been home sick for a while, which explained why the music had suddenly gone away. Upon hearing this, King Hùng rushed his messengers to the village to fetch Trương-Chi and his flute and escort him back to the castle as fast as they could.

"When the young fisherman arrived at the royal court, the king ordered him to play his flute as he normally would at the end of his workday. As the music started to rise, a hush fell over the crowd. No one moved or made a noise, as if a spell had been cast with the beautiful notes from the simple instrument. High up in the tower, the princess heard the music, too. She rose from her bed and asked to be helped down to the large hall where all the people in the castle had gathered to listen. But when Mỵ-Nương laid eyes on the homely fisherman clothed in rags, a change took place in her that she did not understand. The music suddenly lost its magical hold on her while at the same time, her illness began to lift. The princess felt no desire to listen anymore. She quietly turned and headed back to her room at the top of the tower.

"From that day on, Mỵ-Nương no longer waited by her window at sunset for the sound of the flute, and life resumed its normal course at the castle of King Hùng. For the poor fisherman, however, life changed from the moment he caught a glimpse of the beautiful princess. After receiving a reward for his trouble, Trương-Chi returned to his hut on the water's edge but could not stop thinking about Mỵ-Nương. Day and night, he saw her lovely face before his eyes, even in his sleep. Soon, he fell sick again, and this time his health declined rapidly. When winter arrived, and the north wind brought a severe cold to the valley, the young fisherman passed away. His father buried him with his flute under a weeping willow near the water.

"The following spring, the river rose and threatened to flood, so the old man prepared to move his son's grave to higher ground. A big surprise awaited him when he dug into the earth:

There, among his son's remains, he discovered a smooth and shiny rock of flesh-tone color in the place of Trương-Chi's heart. Baffled and shaken by his unusual find, at a loss for what to do, the old man hurried down to the castle where he presented the king with the glossy stone and related the unique circumstances behind it. King Hùng was so touched by the story, he handed the stone to his finest artisan to carve a ceremonial teacup out of it, for all to admire.

"But no one could have foreseen what happened next.

"When the king poured hot tea into the cup, an image slowly formed on its steamy surface. To the shock and disbelief of everyone present, it showed a trembling reflection of Trương-Chi playing the flute while sailing his boat at sunset. Word of the miracle quickly spread through the castle. When the young princess heard about it, she came down from the tower to see for herself. As Mỵ-Nương peered in amazement at the wavering image in the teacup, she suddenly heard the sound of Trương-Chi's flute in her ears—that magical music that had brought her such joy and happiness not too long ago, but now sad and tender, like the story of his broken heart.

"In that moment, the princess's heart broke, too. Tears rolled down her cheeks, and as the warm teardrops fell in the cup, the young fisherman's reflection shattered and disappeared."

Kimmie has remained very still until the end of the story, her eyes full of puzzlement and wonder. She now turns to Grandma, eager to share the one thing she feels certain about. "The princess missed him, *Bà Ngoại*," she declares. "When my cat Tigger died, I cried a long time."

Grandma nods understandingly. "I'm sure you're right, honey," she says. "But I also think the princess had a kind heart, and she knew she could have been nicer to Trương-Chi when she had first met him. Now it was too late, and she felt sorry and very sad for him. And so did I when I was little and my mother first told me the story. I kept begging to hear it over and over again, hoping each time that the ending might be different. So you know what my mother did then?"

Kimmie shakes her bobbed hair, her mouth open in a silent question.

"She brought me back a small gift from the market one day," continues Grandma, smiling wistfully at the childhood memory. "When she placed it in my open hand, I could not believe my eyes. It looked exactly as I had imagined it would." Grandma's head leans down over Kimmie's, gray hair touching black. "Can you guess what it was?"

The child's gaze darts back and forth between Grandma's face and the alabaster teacup on the table, searching for a confirmation clue, then she finally points at the small object before her.

Grandma gives her a big hug. "See how clever you are?" she says warmly. "Yes, this cup here was my mother's gift, and when she saw my eyes open really big, like yours right now, she was quick to correct me that it wasn't the teacup from Trương-Chi. 'But it works the same way,' she went on to assure me. 'So if we ever get separated from each other, Little Candy—that was her baby name for me—remember all you'll need to do is fill this cup with hot tea then think of me, and you'll see me looking right back at you.' " Grandma's voice trails, laden with nostalgia.

"Did you, *Bà Ngoại*? Did you ever try?" Kimmie cries excitedly. "Did it work?"

Grandma breathes a sigh. "You know, honey, I never got to try it out as a kid because my mother was always there for my brother and me while we were growing up. So I played with the cup for a while, and then I just set it aside and completely forgot about it when I grew older." She pauses momentarily. "Until years later."

Sensing another story on the way, Kimmie sits up and grasps her grandmother's hand in eager silence.

"You already know *Bà Ngoại* grew up far away from here, in that ancient land where the legend of Trương-Chi and My-Nương came from. It's all the way on the other side of the world, where it is hot and rainy, with plenty of jungles and rivers. But there are large cities, too, and rice fields everywhere. I lived with my parents and my baby brother in a tiny house in the largest city over there, called Sài-Gòn. It was where I spent all my young life until I grew up and met *Ông Ngoại* and we got married and moved into our own little house."

Grandma feels Kimmie's fingers softly curled around hers, so loving and trusting that her heart melts with tenderness. It does not seem all that long ago that she was dreaming of such a sweet child to call her own while pregnant with Kimmie's mother. Oh, how wonderful life had felt then, not in any material sense—far from it—but as a young wife in love and a first-time expecting mother. The future stretched bright and clear in front of her and Grandpa, as limitless as the horizon after a monsoon downpour. Nothing at all could have thwarted its hopeful promise for the young couple, not even the persistent rumblings of war.

It was at Tết 1975, the traditional Vietnamese New Year's, when Grandma announced the blissful news to their families. A couple of years into their marriage, she and Grandpa had just received the doctor's confirmation that she was indeed expecting. The news, of course, brought a whirlwind of excitement and happiness all around—the first baby in either family in decades. It also provided everybody with a much welcome diversion from mounting worries about the war. Fierce fighting had broken out anew all over the country despite the Paris Peace Accords signed barely two years earlier, and Grandma's younger brother, then an officer in the South Vietnamese Army, had not been granted leave to come home for Tết.

But even those inauspicious circumstances could do little to dampen the joy of budding motherhood that was overflowing in her. Every day of that first week of the Year of the Cat, following her announcement, she and her mother donned their traditional silk *áo dài* and trekked to one pagoda after another around the city—their New Year's pilgrimage. At each temple, they added their offerings of yellow mums and fresh fruit to the large altar, lit big sticks of incense, and prayed to Buddha and the ancestors with all their hearts: her mother for her brother's safety, and she for her unborn baby's good health. Under shimmering candle-light, suffused in incense fragrance and the meditative sounds of wooden bells and gongs, she felt for the first time an intimate bond with that precious life inside her belly.

Kimmie wiggles her fingers free from Grandma's to fiddle with her hair ribbon. "But where are your mommy and daddy now, *Bà Ngoại?*" she asks with a puzzled frown. "Does your baby brother live with them?"

Holding the little girl close, Grandma rests her chin lightly atop Kimmie's head. The child's innocent questions stir up a swirl of memories and drag her further down a path she hesitates to follow. But already, the mist of nostalgia is clouding her eyes as her mind drifts back to an earlier lifetime, in a world on fire: those cataclysmic days and months in early 1975.

The year had started out so blessed and propitious for her and Grandpa, first with him landing a coveted job at an American bank in Sài-Gòn, followed soon by the news of their first baby on its way. Sure, everybody was on edge about the war blazing again, but that was hardly a new development. Such had been the way of life for their generation as well as their parents' and grandparents'. And so, despite all the fighting, the young couple was brimming with joy and gratitude for their simple blessings and holding great hopes for the future.

Until, overnight, their entire world was torn down all around them.

In March of that year, the U.S., mired in economic recession and the political aftermath of Watergate, announced to the world it had put the war behind it. All American aid to South Việt-Nam, military or otherwise, was summarily terminated, regardless of consequences. That left the fledgling democracy defenseless and wide open to the advancing Communists from the north, who had the total and unwavering support of the Soviet Union and Red China. Panic and despair swept the whole country and plunged it into feverish chaos as never seen before. Terrified of being abandoned to the enemy, South Vietnamese soldiers and civilians stampeded out of the northern provinces to flee south to the relative safety of Sài-Gòn. Meanwhile, inside the capital itself, people watched the catastrophe play out on TV news in stunned horror and helplessness, sensing the noose of war tightening each day around their own haven.

Grandma hugs Kimmie tighter. "You see, sweetie, someday when you grow up and have your own family, you may have to move away from the place you've lived all your life, away from your parents and other people you love."

"But I don't want to," the little girl protests.

"Sometimes it just happens, baby," Grandma says, soft as a sigh. "As it happened to *Ông Ngoại* and me many years ago, when we had to leave our families and our home in Việt-Nam."

April in Sài-Gòn usually means the beginning of summer and happy times, with the return of the monsoon showers that bring out luscious red blooms on poinciana trees all over the city. But April 1975 was aflame with artillery fire as North Vietnamese tanks thundered toward the capital, and the threat of a final carnage hung like a deathly pall over the city. People with means had already fled the country, while the rest circled in panic, scrambling to find a last-minute escape. Even now, decades later, Grandma's insides still knot at the memory of feeling trapped—that paralyzing fear and hopelessness as the end loomed ever nearer.

She can never forget that day in April 1975 when Grandpa rushed home at noon from the American bank downtown where he worked. Without a word, he scurried to shut the front door and all the windows before sitting her down at the kitchen table.

"We must hurry and pack," he said breathlessly, his jaws set tight and his forehead dripping with sweat. "One suitcase each. We're leaving in a couple of hours."

"Where . . ." Grandma could not even finish the question, her voice suddenly deserting her.

"My bank, they received permission to evacuate the employees to America." Grandpa blew air out through his cracked lips. Then the details came tumbling out in one big rush. "There's a pickup place downtown we need to get to before five this afternoon. The bus leaves right on the hour for Tân-Sơn-Nhất Airport, so we must be there on time. And not a word to anybody. If this leaks out, we'll be mobbed, and the whole thing will be called off."

They stared speechlessly at each other, eyes wild, hearts pounding so furiously Grandma thought her eardrums might burst. *This* was the miraculous lifeline they had been praying for in recent weeks. Everyone knew the grim fate awaiting those who had "collaborated" with the Americans, the instant the Communists took over. It was widely believed that there would be a bloodbath of retribution countless times worse than the massacre in Huế during the 1968 Tết Offensive. So this was indeed their last, their one and only chance at self-preservation.

And yet—and yet she was overcome with terror instead of relief.

"What about your parents?" Grandma could barely get the words out, so tight and parched her throat was. Her hands were shaking beyond control; she had to pull them down into her lap and keep them there. She swallowed again. "What about . . . mine?"

Grandpa dropped his head under her pleading gaze, his voice a resigned whisper. "We can't bring them. It's employees and their spouses and children only."

She started crying but bit down on her lip to stifle the sobs. Time, suddenly the rarest of commodities, was fast slipping away as they were dawdling. "You must at least go say goodbye to your parents," she told Grandpa through the tears, pushing him toward the door. "Go now. Go. I will pack, and then I will run to go see mine. I won't leave without speaking to them." Like the majority of households in Sài-Gòn at the time, theirs wasn't routed for a telephone line.

They had made preparations for an emergency like this—a necessary habit in wartime—so it did not take her long to pack.

Besides, how much of a life can one really squeeze into a couple of suitcases? Then, staggering in a great hurry through the frenzied streets of a city in its death gasps, she somehow managed to arrive at her parents' house in short order. One look at her haggard face, and they were right by her side. Each holding her by an arm, they helped her into the front room, where she slumped down into a chair.

Between sobs, Grandma struggled to explain the situation to her parents, who listened in stunned silence. In the midst of the agitation, a wild idea struck her. "Why don't you both come with us?" she said, suddenly animated with brazen hope. "Go pack now. Quick. They . . . they can't possibly turn you away once you show up. There's just no way. I will beg them. We will give them all the money, everything we have. I will—"

Her father grasped her hands, shook them gently as he tried to calm her down. "You know they only have so many seats on the plane. Also, your mother and I must stay here and wait for news from your brother. We have not heard from him for days now. . . ." His voice quivered despite a reassuring smile on his face. "Don't worry. We'll be fine. But you and your husband must get out of here."

Her mother, who had dashed into the bedroom for a moment, returned to her side. Fighting to steady her trembling hands, she hung a gold necklace with a pendant around Grandma's neck. "This is for protection and good luck . . ." she started, then choked up. Grandma recognized the small jade pendant of Quan-Âm, the Goddess of Compassion, a relic of love from her deceased grandmother to her mother. Now hastily passed on to her—her farewell gift. They embraced in tears, clinging to each other in despair, for just one minute more. She felt her mother's hand stroking her hair, so tender and loving, just like in her childhood days.

Her father gently pulled them apart, then guided her, limp in his arms, to the door. His eyes were red, his brave smile twitching slightly. "Go, go," he said in a hoarse voice, yanking the door open for her. "Don't miss the plane. May you both travel safely wherever you go. Be happy and take good care of our grandchild."

"Wait. Wait a minute." Grandma heard her mother's voice rising in panic, felt the rustling of her blouse as she frantically brushed past her father to reach her, and then a small, round object being pushed into her hand. "Keep it. Remember . . ." was all her mother could utter in that final moment at the door, before letting go of her hand. The last image Grandma caught of her parents, which was burned indelibly into her memory, was of them leaning against each other outside the doorstep of her childhood home, waving goodbye as they stood and watched their daughter stumble away—forever out of their lives.

Distraught and in shock, it wasn't until she made it home that Grandma realized what it was she gripped in her hand. Her favorite plaything from younger years, long since forgotten: the Trương-Chi teacup. She had had no idea her parents had held on to it all that time, and in a flash, she understood her mother's last words to her.

Grandma straightens the bow in Kimmie's hair. "It was such a crazy time when *Ông Ngoại* and I had to leave our home in Việt-Nam. There was no possible way we could bring our parents and my brother along with us, as badly as we wanted to. The only keepsakes I have of them are the teacup and this necklace. That's why these things are very special to me."

The little girl twists around as Grandma holds out the necklace for her to get a good look at. Eyes bright with curiosity, Kimmie runs her finger back and forth over the jade pendant. "You miss them a lot, don't you, *Bà Ngoại?*" she asks.

The old woman leans over, wraps both her arms tightly around her granddaughter.

There are just no words to explain to anyone, let alone an innocent young child, how much she has missed the family she left behind—the agony of separation, the regrets and survivor's guilt, the struggle to build a life in the new homeland. She and Grandpa waited two long years after their last-minute evacuation from Sài-Gòn in April 1975 before they dared write home to their parents, for fear of causing them unwitting trouble with the Communist regime. Only then did Grandma begin to learn, in bits and pieces dribbled out cautiously through postal mail that they suspected was censored, what her loved ones had endured in the interim.

Her brother had been captured by the North Vietnamese during the last days of fighting and later sent to a remote "reeducation camp" in the highlands in the north. It took her parents much effort and many a costly bribe to locate where he was held.

Once a year from then on, either her father or her mother would undertake the days-long journey to go visit their imprisoned son and bring him a few meager comforts from home: small jars of preserved foods, mended clothes or a used sweater, and most importantly, what precious quinine pills they could smuggle in to help ease his bouts with malaria and dysentery. Grandma would send letters for her brother and what little savings she could scrape up to her parents' address, and they would always share his latest news with her after each annual trek to the "reeducation" camp in the mountains.

But then one day, when Grandma's mother arrived at the camp, she was made to wait around at the visitors' station for an unusually long time. In the end, a stone-faced comrade appeared and informed her that her son had passed away from an "accident" months earlier. Then the man had her sign some forms, which she did in a sleepwalking-like state, before he released to her a small bag of her son's personal effects—all that was left of him.

The shock and pain of that devastating loss, on top of economic hardship and severe deprivation, sent Grandma's parents on a downward spiral from which they never recovered. Within five years of her brother's untimely death, they too passed on, first her mother, followed shortly by her father. Ironically, it all happened not long before she and Grandpa were granted U.S. citizenship, which would have allowed them to start the immigration paperwork to bring her parents to America.

Losing her homeland and then all her loved ones within a span of a few years proved too great a blow for Grandma to withstand. There were times when she felt she could no longer go on. If it had not been for the devoted love and support of Grandpa and the fact that Kimmie's mother, then just a young child, needed her desperately, she might simply have given up.

Grandma draws a deep breath before slowly letting it out. "I never got to see my parents or my brother again after we left Việt-Nam," she says softly. "They died a short time after we were gone. But there is not a day goes by that I don't think of them and miss them."

Kimmie senses her great sadness. The little girl turns, reaches up with her small arms, and throws them around her grandmother's neck. "I love you, *Bà Ngoại*," she says.

Eyes closed to stem the wave of emotions, Grandma presses her cheek against Kimmie's. "I love you, too, sweetheart—so, so much," she whispers in the little girl's ear.

Taking a moment to compose herself, she then goes on in a lighter tone, "My mother knew I would be terribly homesick. That's why she gave me the teacup to take with me when I left. I am sure you already know what I was supposed to do with it, don't you?"

"Yes, yes, *Bà Ngoại*," cries Kimmie. "Did you pour tea and look inside?"

Grandma smiles ruefully and reaches for the cup, twirling it slowly in her fingers. "Any time I missed my parents and baby brother and felt sad, I would come in here, make some fresh tea, and pour myself a cup. And I still do."

Kimmie sits up and stares into the half-full cup. "*Bà Ngoại ơi*, did you ever see something?"

Grandma kisses the back of her head before answering, "You want to hear a secret?"

As the child nods in earnest and promptly settles back in her chair, Grandma begins, "It's a wonderful thing I discovered a long time ago. Whenever you remember someone you loved, no matter how long after they have gone, it's like they are with you once again—right here." She affectionately taps on Kimmie's chest. "All you need to do then is sit still, close your eyes, and think of all the fun times you had with them. And then you will be able to see them in your head. This teacup helps remind me of all the great memories I shared with my parents and my baby brother when he and I were growing up. Do you know what I call it?"

Kimmie shakes her head uncertainly, a finger resting on her dimpled chin.

"I call it my cup of love," Grandma says. "Every time I drink tea from it, I can almost see and hear my mother telling us the story of Trương-Chi and My-Nương all those years ago. And it makes me feel warm and happy inside. Just like we were all together again." She gives Kimmie a tickle in the ribs. "And now, baby girl, you know all my secrets."

Laughing in delight, Kimmie snuggles up to Grandma, who gently strokes her hair before continuing, "Someday, when I'm gone, I want you and your mommy to have my teacup."

The little girl seizes her grandmother's hand. "No, *Bà Ngoại*. I don't want you to die."

"I don't plan to go anywhere anytime soon, honey," Grandma says, pulling Kimmie closer to her. "We are having too much fun together yet. But suppose I have to go away for a few days, and you miss me, you will know just what to do now, won't you?"

"I will ask Mommy to make tea and pour it in the cup. And then . . . and then we will sit right here. I will tell her all of your stories."

"Atta girl," says Grandma with a chuckle. "But you know what, honey? I think *Ông Ngoại* will be home anytime now, and he will be tickled pink to see you. Let me get his plate and fork so he can share these delicious mung bean cookies with us."

As Grandma slowly gets up from the table, Kimmie seems deep in thought.

"*Bà Ngoại ơi,*" she finally says, "how old was Mommy then?"

"When *Ông Ngoại* and I left Việt-Nam? Hmm. Let's see. She was . . . quite small."

"Smaller than me?"

"Oh, sure. She was just an itsy-bitsy little thing." Grandma smiles as she sets the extra plate and fork down on the table. "So tiny, in fact, she was able to fit comfortably inside my tummy."

Kimmie's mouth drops open. "Oh, *Bà Ngoại*, tell me, tell me more, please!"

"That's a whole other story for another time, sweetie," says Grandma, a twinkle in her eyes.

About the Author

C. L. Hoàng was born and raised in Việt-Nam during the war and came to the United States in the 1970s. He graduated from the University of California, Berkeley, and earns his living as an electronic engineer, with eleven patents to his name. His first book, *Once upon a Mulberry Field*, is an award-winning novel set in Việt-Nam at the height of the war. It is followed by *Rain Falling on Tamarind Trees*, a travelogue of his 2016 visit to the ancestral homeland and a former Amazon #1 New Release in Việt-Nam Travel Guides. *In the Shadow of Green Bamboos* is his latest publication.

www.mulberryfieldsforever.com

CPSIA information can be obtained
at www.ICGtesting.com
Printed in the USA
BVHW031528141020
591013BV00001B/62